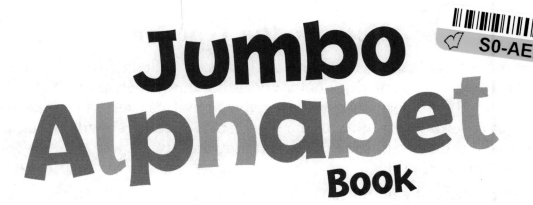

Contents

Carson-Dellosa Publishing, LLC
Greensboro, North Carolina

Notes to the Teacher

- You may wish to begin with some of the letter A activities and discover what pace works best for your class before deciding how much time you will spend on each section. If you decide to use only a few activities from each section, you may be able to cover a letter section in a day or two. If children will be completing all or nearly all the activities included, you may find that it will take a week or more to cover each section.

- The second page of each letter section has a full-page pattern that matches the letter. It can be used with oral activities, it can be copied and used by the students for coloring or writing practice (on the front of the car), or you can assemble a "train" using all 26 pattern pages on a wall or bulletin board. The patterns can also be used as labels in the room or as student awards.

- Feel free to modify the use of the patterns included in this book to suit your classroom needs. The *Jumbo Alphabet Book* has numerous patterns and their use should not be limited to the accompanying activities or directions. Patterns can also be used for mobiles, coloring activities, puzzles, bulletin board displays, and more.

Caution: Before beginning any nature activity, ask families' permission and inquire about students' plant and animal allergies. Remind students not to touch plants or animals during the activity.

Caution: Before beginning any food activity, ask families' permission and inquire about students' food allergies and religious or other food restrictions.

Carson-Dellosa Publishing, LLC
PO Box 35665
Greensboro, NC 27425 USA
carsondellosa.com

3

"A" Vocabulary and Oral Expression

Introducing "A"

Introduce "a" words through conversation, illustrations, and questions. (What makes you angry? What would you put in an aquarium? Have you ever heard of Alaska and Africa?)

Foods	Names		Animals	Careers
apples	Amy	Andy	alligator	accountant
apricots	Ann	Alice	ape	actor
asparagus	Andrew	Arlene	ant	actress
avocado	Adam	Audrey	anteater	astronaut
almonds	Alex	Aaron	angel fish	astronomer
angel food cake	Abby	Alan	armadillo	artist
artichoke	Archie	Albert	aardvark	architect
	April	Alvin		author
	Arnold	Arthur		

"A" Opposites

Ask students to tell the opposites of these "a" words:

after	all
alike	awake
alive	above

You may also give other words and ask students to tell "a" words which are opposite of the words you name:

before	none
different	asleep
dead	below

"A" Objects

Ask, "Can you tell me about any of the following things?" (Make a note of those things that no one can describe and provide pictures at a later date.)

accordion	apron	ax
acorn	airplane	anchor
anklet	antenna	awning
arrow	acrobat	apartment

Tongue Twisters

- Ask children to repeat in unison after you. Then ask if anyone would like to try to say a tongue twister as fast as possible alone.

Alex is absent again. *Astronaut Al's airplane arrived.*
Alan Arnold acts angry. *Almost all the apricots are alike.*
Amy always asks for apples. *Arlene and Aaron are afraid of ants.*
Alligators are ancient animals.

- Now ask students to add one or more "a" words to the following to make tongue twisters:

Alice ate...
Austin's aunt...
Artie always...
Arnold Ant adds...
All the apes are...

- Tell children to answer "yes" or "no" to these questions and to explain why they answered as they did.

Can alphabets add? *Can an ambulance arrive?*
Can your Aunt Amy argue? *Can ashes aim arrows?*
Can antlers be angry? *Can an athlete applaud?*
Can an airplane appear? *Is an anteater aqua?*

"A" Art and Activities

Animal Cracker Art

Materials: animal crackers (enough so each child can have three or four for the project and some to eat)
glue
construction paper
crayons or markers

Discuss animal habitats (jungle, field, zoo, forest, farm, city, etc.). Give the children the animal crackers. Tell them to select two or more to glue on the paper. Then have them draw around the animals to show where they might live.

Use Your Senses

Senses of Touch and Smell:
1. Duplicate the letter "A" on page 3.
2. Cover it with glue. Sprinkle with allspice or cinnamon.
3. Have students close their eyes, then feel and smell the page.

Sense of Taste
Have an "a" tasting day. Ask parents for donations of foods whose names begin with "a." Let students try avocados, asparagus, apricots, almonds, and artichokes.

Sense of Hearing
Ask students to think of "alarming" noises to imitate (i.e., alarm clock, fire alarm, ambulance, fire engine, smoke detector, etc.).

Sense of Sight
Play "I Spy." When children are out of the room, place items beginning with the letter "a" in clear view (apple, airplane, toy animals, apron, etc.). When students return, begin a game by saying, "I spy an 'a' object in the room..." and give a clue to its identity (i.e., "...that you might wear while cooking"). The student who guesses correctly may then say "I spy." An adult may need to whisper a suggestion for an object or clue.

Apple Day

- Ask everyone to bring an apple on Apple Day. Be sure to have some extras on hand for children who forget or aren't able to obtain one. Place them together and compare colors, taste, texture, etc.
- Let students count the number of seeds in their apples. Have each student compare with others. Which apples have the most seeds? Which have the fewest? Are there any which have the same number?

- Cut some apples in half as shown at right. Let children press them flesh side down onto an ink pad or paint which has been rolled out on a pan. Have students press the apple halves on paper. Did they form stars?

- Eat apples or Apple Sandwiches (recipe, page 15) at snack time.
- At the end of the day, give each child at least one of the apple awards on page 9.
- On apple day, share books like the following with your students:
  Ten Apples Up on Top, by Theodore LeSieg. Random House, 1988.
  The Apple Tree, by Lynley Dodd. Gareth Stevens, 1985.

WHAT CAN WE COOK USING APPLES?

Baked Apples   Candy Apples
Apple Pie   Apple Sandwiches
Apple Sauce   Apple Butter

Apple Awards

Some ideas for these awards are "You are the apple of my eye because...," "An apple from your teacher because...," and "I know the letter 'A'."

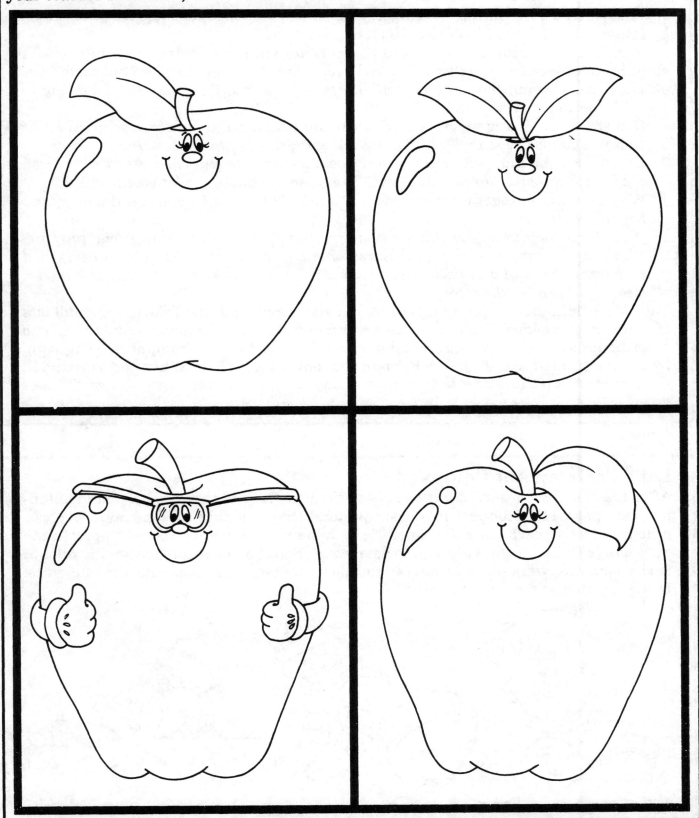

9

"A" Science

Let's Take a Look at Ants

A good book for introducing the subject of ants is *Questions and Answers about Ants*, by Millicent E. Selsam (Scholastic Book Services, 1967).

Pass around pictures of ants and several jars with one or two ants in each for children to observe as you discuss ants. If you are able to purchase an ant farm, it is excellent for viewing the habits of these insects. Use questions like the following in class discussion:

- Can you count how many body sections an ant has? *(An ant has three body sections.)*
- Can you count the ant's legs? *(An ant has six legs; all true insects do.)*
- Do you see the ants' antennae? *(Describe antennae for students. When ants meet, they touch antennae to communicate. They also use antennae for smelling.)*
- Why do ants live together in colonies, or hills? *(They work together, share food, and help each other.)*
- What kinds of jobs do you think ants might have? *(Each ant has a special purpose. There is a queen who lays eggs; nurse ants which care for the queen's eggs; food gatherers who find and gather food for the colony; and worker ants which enlarge, clean, and protect the colony.)*

Take some hand-held magnifying lenses and visit some ant hills. Take along small bits of crackers or cookies. Sprinkle them around and see what happens. Ask students to describe an ant hill (they may wonder where the sand comes from; ants bring it up from underground in their jaws). Explain that ants hibernate together underground in the winter. Ask if the students see wings on any of the ants (males have wings; females do not).

Let's Form an Ant Colony

After the class has observed ant behavior, direct each child to make headband antennae (see page 11). Students may then pretend they are ants in a colony. They can practice meeting each other and smelling with their antennae. The boys can pretend to have wings while the girls pretend to have none. Select a queen and assign the roles of food gatherers, workers, and nurses to other students. Let students pretend to be living together and doing their jobs.

Antennae Headband Pattern

Have students color and cut out the patterns below. Headband pieces can be sized to student's head and stapled or taped end-to-end to form a band. Antennae can be attached as in the illustration on page 10.

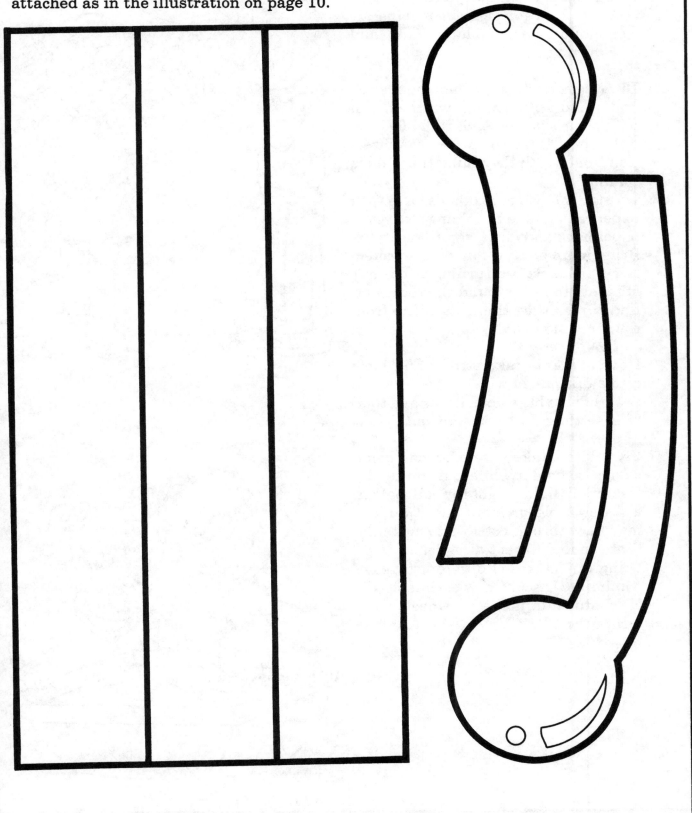

Learn about Air

Use your eyes:

Ask students to use their eyes as you take a walk and look for signs of moving air (flags, clouds, leaves, long hair, and clothes moving).

Feel air:

• Direct students to extend their arms and stand still. Then have them run with their arms extended and feel the difference. Have them face the direction from which they think the wind is coming.

• Let students fan each other's faces with paper fans (made by folding a sheet of paper back and forth, accordion style).

• Bring in an electric fan with a protective shield. Before turning it on, ask students to look around the room and find things they think the wind from the fan will move.

Use air:

• Have students take straws and blow into a dishpan of water.

• Let students blow up balloons and then release them to let the air out. What happens?

• Fly a kite. Make sure everyone has a chance to hold it while it is in the air.

• Use small, lightweight toy sailboats in a water table or large tub. Children may blow through straws to make the boats go in different directions.

• Bring in pictures of different types of windmills. Discuss how each is used.

• Help students make pinwheels (pattern, page 13).

12

Pinwheel Pattern

Give each student a copy of the pinwheel pattern below. Have them color both sides of the square and then cut along all the solid lines. Bend each corner marked with a small circle over the center of the pinwheel until it overlaps the larger circle. Poke a thumbtack or pin through the four corners and pinwheel middle into the eraser on the end of a pencil. The pinwheel will turn as air is blown into it.

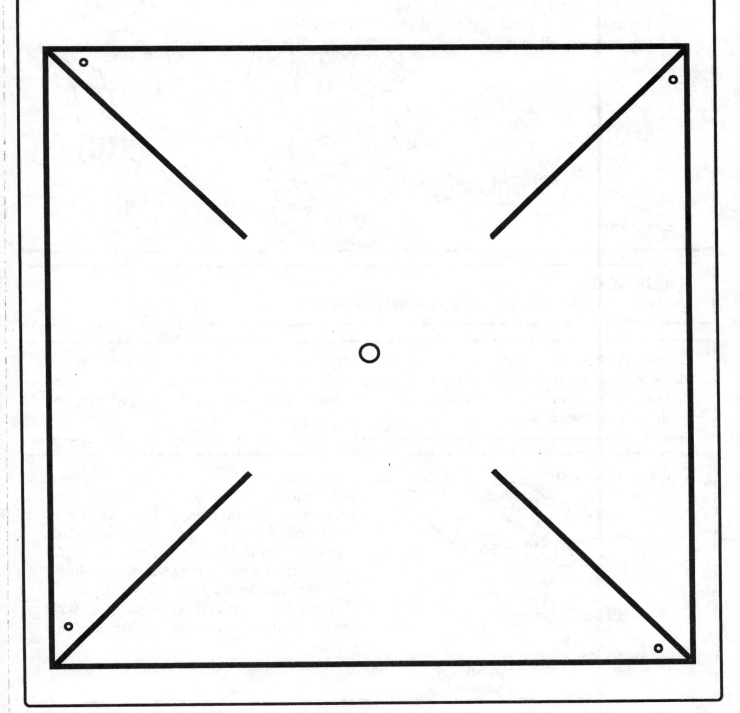

"A" Movement

Animal Walks

Have students walk to a line and back (or in a circle) as you name the following animals for them to imitate:

elephant— bend over, make arms swing like trunk, clasp hands
duck—squat and waddle
crab—on all fours face up, walk backward or sideways
rabbit—hop, put arms between legs before each hop
penguin—arms stiff, feet pointed out
kangaroo—jump with feet together and arms folded
frog—leap on all fours

Ankle Walk

Let students walk to a line and back holding their ankles.

Be an Acrobat

Have students pretend they are walking a tightrope (use a balance beam or a line drawn on the floor). Let them do simple gymnastics like somersaults, body rolls, and beginning cartwheels.

Be an Airplane

Ask students to be on the ground, start their engines, taxi on the runway, wait for the okay from the tower, take off, climb high, fly, see the landing runway, call for permission to land, bring the planes down, and taxi to the airport. Children can do this activity with their bodies or with model planes made with glue and ice cream sticks.

"A" Foods

Apple Sandwiches

For snack time on Apple Day or any day, prepare apple sandwiches with students.

Materials: one apple for every two to three children
a sharp knife for cutting
a few dull knives for spreading
apple corer
simple sandwich fillings (i.e., peanut butter, cheese, honey, raisins)

Core each apple and cut off the top and bottom. Slice into rings about ½ inch thick. Use two rings like bread. Have children fill by spreading their favorite fillings on the rings.

Apple Juice

You will need: ¾ cup of pared, sliced apples
1 cup water
1 teaspoon sugar (less if the apples are very sweet)
a blender

Combine all the ingredients and blend. Chill, strain if necessary, and enjoy.

Applesauce

You will need: 4 pounds tart cooking apples
½ cup sugar
½ teaspoon cinnamon or a few red cinnamon candies
1 cup water
1 tablespoon lemon juice

Pare, core, and thinly slice apples. Add the water and lemon juice. Cover and cook on low heat until very soft. Add cinnamon and sugar; stir. Cool.

Candied Apples

You will need: 2 pounds vanilla caramels
6 tablespoons hot water
12 medium apples
12 ice cream sticks

Melt the caramels and water on top of a double boiler over boiling water. Stir until they form a smooth sauce. Wash, dry, and remove stems from apples. Insert an ice cream stick into the blossom end of each apple. Remove the sauce from the heat. Hold each apple by the stick and dip into the sauce, coating the entire surface. If the sauce becomes too thick, add a little water. Place the apples, stick side up, on buttered wax paper and refrigerate until time to eat. (Variation: After covering with caramel, roll the apples in chopped nuts and/or candy sprinkles.)

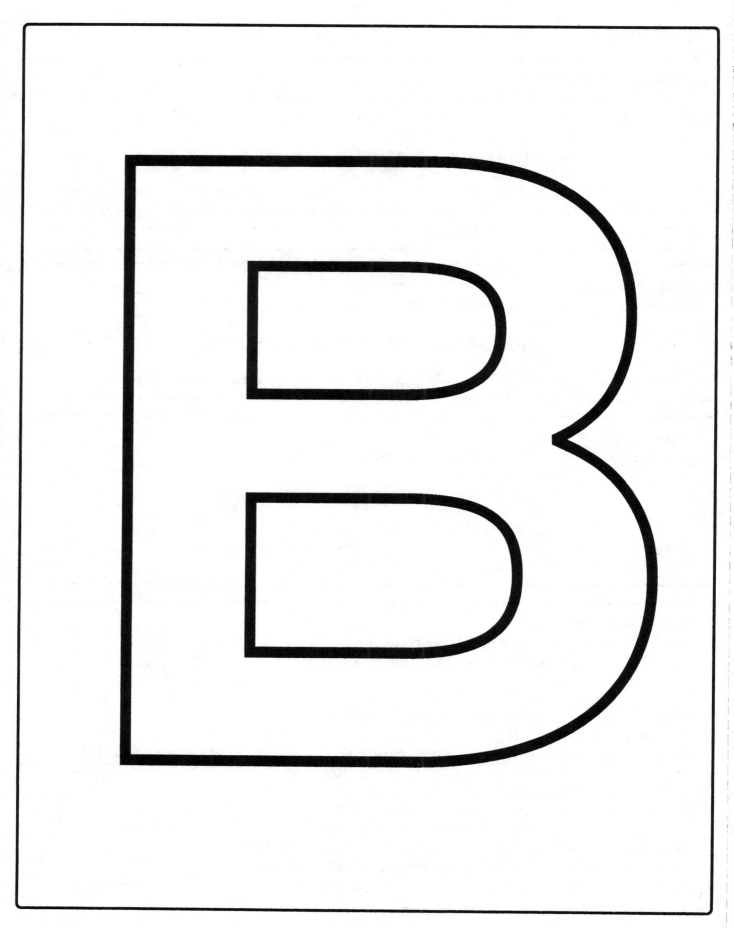

16

© Carson-Dellosa • CD-104781

17

"B" Vocabulary and Oral Expression

Introducing "B"

Introduce "b" words through conversation, illustrations, and questions. (Did you ever walk over a bridge? Have you ever seen a blimp? Where would you look to see buds?)

Foods

bacon	bread
banana	butter
beans	buns
beet	bologna
beef	berries
biscuits	bagels
broccoli	

Names

Barbara	Bert
Beth	Billy
Bess	Bobby
Beverly	Brian
Bonnie	Brett
Brenda	Bruce
Bridget	Brandon
Barney	Brad
Barry	Byron
Benny	Buddy

Animals

badger
beaver
bear
bobcat
bee
butterfly
bird

Careers

butcher
barber
baker
banker
bricklayer

Homonyms

brake-break	bee-be
board-bored	beat-beet
by-buy-bye	blue-blew
bear-bare	beech-beach

"B" Sounds and Actions

Who or what might make these sounds?

boo	bow-wow (bark)
buzz	beep
baa	boom

What do you know that might do these things?

blink	bite
bend	boil
build	

BARK BARK BARK

BAAAAA

"B" Objects

Ask, "Can you tell me about any of the following things?" (Make a note of those things that no one can describe and provide pictures at a later date.)

bush	barn	braid
building	bonnet	bracelet
branch	bugle	buckle
buggy	burlap	beaks

Tongue Twisters

- Ask children to repeat in unison after you. Then ask if anyone would like to try to say a tongue twister as fast as possible alone.

Bonnie Beaver blows bubbles. *Billie Bee busily buzzes.*
Bobby Brown's brother builds boats. *Bert, Billy, and Barney blow bugles.*
Brenda's baby buggy bounces. *Bridget's boyfriend broke his buckle.*

- Now ask students to add one or more "b" words to the following to make tongue twisters:

Bobby Butler bakes.......
Brian's beagle buries.......
Busy Betty Bee........
Brandon brought.........
Bea's big bicycle ....

- Tell children to answer "yes" or "no" to these questions and to explain why they answered as they did.

Can boats button blouses? *Can a bush use a brush?*
Can a brother blow a bugle? *Can a baker bake a bagel?*
Can a bride buy bread? *Can a broom breathe?*
Does a bug wear boots? *Can a book blush?*

"B" Art and Activities

Bean Bag Activities

Bean Bag Toss—Tape numbers, letters, or pictures to the floor. Ask children to try to hit specific ones with their bean bags. (Their age, numbers in their telephone number, address, number of people in their family, the letters in their name, pictures of objects that begin with the letter "b", etc.)

Bean Bag Walk—Have students walk across a balance beam or a line taped on the floor with beanbags on their heads. Let them walk in a circle or around the room listening to music. Suggest places to put the beanbags and let students try to balance them while they walk (head, shoulder, top of outstretched hand, etc.).

Use Your Senses

Senses of Touch and Smell
1. Duplicate the letter "B" on page 16.
2. Cover it with glue. Lay dried beans, uncooked barley, basil, or strips of burlap on the letter.
3. Have students close their eyes, then feel the page. They may also smell it if they used barley or basil.

Sense of Taste
Have a "b" tasting day. Ask parents for donations of foods whose names begin with "b." Serve various types of beans, breads, and berries (blueberries, if possible). Let students try bean sprouts, beets, broccoli and Brussels sprouts.

Sense of Hearing
Review the "b" sounds on page 18. Ask children to raise their hands if they can name something that might make that sound.

Sense of Sight
When children are out of the room, place items beginning with the letter "b" in clear view (blackboard, books, bulletin board, boxes, balls, bears, blankets, balance beam, etc.). When students return, begin a game by saying, "I spy a 'b' object in the room..." and give a clue to its identity (i.e., "...that you might use with chalk"). The student who guesses correctly may then say "I spy." An adult may need to whisper a suggestion for an object or clue.

Bear Day

- Everyone brings a teddy bear to school on this day. Have a few extra that can be adopted for the day by those who forget.
- Plan a teddy bear's picnic near trees if you have them in your schoolyard or have one in a pretend woods in your classroom.
- Have the bears sing, dance, run races, do somersaults, stand on their heads, and tell jokes (with the help of the owners). Make sure each bear wins a ribbon or prize before the day is over. Refreshments of bear cookies and "berry" good punch can be served. Children might enjoy telling something interesting or special about their bears.

Bubble Blow

This is best done outdoors.

You will need: 1 quart of warm water
¾ cup dishwashing detergent
⅓ cup glycerine (available in drugstores)
bubble makers (straws, funnels, slotted spoons, coat
hangers or any other material bent into a circle)

You might have children take turns being the judge and at any given moment call out the name of the person who has the biggest bubble.

Beanbags

Children will enjoy making their own beanbags.

You will need: 2 squares of plain material per child
(a cut-up old sheet will work)
markers and crayons for decorating
dried beans for filling

Have children decorate both squares of fabric. An adult should sew the squares together (with the designs on the inside) leaving a one to two inch opening. (Use a sewing machine, if possible.) Children can then turn their squares right-side out and fill loosely with beans. The openings can be sewn shut or temporarily closed with safety pins until time allows the holes to be sewn. Bean bags can be used for a variety of activities.

Button Match

You will need pairs of matching buttons for this activity. Sew or paste one button from each pair to a card. Mix and put all the remaining buttons in the middle of a table. Children can work in small groups to see how fast they can match up the buttons by laying the matching one beside its mate.

Backward Day

Send notes home to parents telling them that tomorrow will be backward day. Their child may wear one item of clothing backwards. (Best choices are blouses, shirts, and sweaters.) Whenever possible and safe, do things backwards during the day (line up, walk, sit, etc.).

Bakery

Visit a bakery. Have a pretend bakery in the classroom. Sell real or pretend bread, biscuits, buns, and bagels.

Bowling

If you do not have classroom pins, you can set up used quart milk cartons, detergent bottles, or tall potato chip cans. (Put a few rocks or sand in each one to make it stable.) Children may set up the pins in any pattern they wish and roll (not throw) a large, heavy ball to see how many they can knock down. Then ask,"How many are still up? How many did you knock down?"

Birdseed "B"

Give each child a container of birdseed. In the yard (outside your window if possible), have each child spread his seed on the ground or snow in the shape of a capital B. Watch the birds come for breakfast or brunch.

Bare Feet Fun

Have children remove their socks and shoes and work with partners. Each child stands on a sheet of paper while the partner draws the outline of her feet. The feet can then be colored, cut out, and taped around the room to look like they are walking places—maybe even up a wall! Children will have fun looking for their feet.

Blue, Black and Brown Days

Have one day set aside for each color. Ask children to wear clothing of that color. Have children draw, cut out, and paste on a mural pictures of objects that are the color of the day.

Balloon Activities

Balloon Volleyball—Run a ribbon across the room about a foot higher than your tallest child. Pair up the children and give each pair a balloon. They are to bat the balloon back and forth across the ribbon with their hands.

Balloon Bat—Give every child a balloon. Explain that each child should try to keep his balloon from touching the floor by batting it with his hands. Children should stop and hold their balloons when they hear you ring a bell until it is rung a second time.

Button Pictures

Send notes home asking for donations of unwanted buttons. Ask children to draw pictures that include things with circles (such as a T.V. set with knobs, clothing with buttons, traffic light, etc.). Then glue buttons over the circles.

If you have pairs of buttons left, use them for the button match game on page 23.

Blindfold Art

Tape three or four large sheets of paper to the chalkboard or let students use chalk and draw directly on the chalkboard. Put students into groups of three or four. Decide on a "B" object that every group will draw and blindfold each child before he goes up to draw. If, for example, the object to be drawn is a bear, the first child may be asked to draw the body and the head. The second will draw the ears and the eyes; next, the nose and the arms, etc. Each group's finished creation can then be displayed and signed by all the artists. Children will have fun with their blindfold art.

Blot Butterflies

You will need: copies of the butterfly outline (page 26)
tempera paints (all colors)
paint brushes
pipe cleaners cut into 2 inch sections (optional)

Duplicate and cut out one copy of the butterfly outline for each child. Direct them to fold the outline on the dashed line, open again, and paint one side only. Refold immediately while paint is still wet and press down on the clean side. Open and glue on pipe cleaners for antennae when dry.

Butterfly Outline

"B" Games

Blindman's Bluff
One child is chosen to be "it" and stands blindfolded in the middle. The rest of the children form a circle around the "blindman" who tells them to walk. He then gives instructions to stop and points in one direction. The child closest to where he is pointing steps forward and takes his hand. The blindman may touch the face, hair and upper body of the unknown person holding his hand and has three guesses who it is. No one should talk. The teacher should say yes or no to the guesses. Right or wrong, there should be a new blindman each time so everyone has a turn.

Button, Button, Who Has the Button?
The person who is "it" closes his eyes. The rest of the children sit very close together in a circle around the person with their hands behind them. Facing the center of the circle, they pass a button (the bigger, the better) behind their backs. Once passing begins, the person in the middle can open his eyes. Everyone should be moving their hands all the time to look like they are passing the button. When the passing stops, the person in the center has three guesses as to who has the button. If correct, the person with the button becomes "it." No one should have more than two turns.

Bell Tag
Mark off a large area in your room or outside. Everyone must stay within this area while playing. (An adult can move any blindfolded players back in if they stray out.) Everyone is blindfolded but the one who carries the bell. This person must ring the bell on every step. The others listen and try to tap the "ringer." If caught, he takes the blindfold and gives his "tapper" the bell.

"B" Foods

Biscuit Bunnies

You will need: refrigerator biscuits
(three for each child)
small foods (such as nuts,
cannies, raisins, cher-
ries, etc.) for making
face features

Place two biscuits together for the head and body. Cut the third one in half to make the ears. Lay the bunny on a cookie sheet and use food bits to make eyes, nose, and mouth. An adult could pull apart an additional biscuit and give a small bit of dough to each child for a tail. Bake according to package directions.

Banana Balls

You will need: one ripe banana for each child
forks
cinnamon
nuts, raisins, cereal bits
chocolate and/or butterscotch chips

Have each child mash a banana, sprinkle in a little cinnamon (demonstrate), roll into balls and press on food bits. Place on wax paper on a cookie sheet (names by each so that they can eat their own) and refrigerate until snack time.

Butterscotch Bars

You will need: 6 cups of any crunchy cereal
1 cup peanut butter
12 ounces butterscotch morsels

Place butterscotch morsels and peanut butter in the top of a double boiler over boiling water and stir until smooth. Remove from heat. Stir in cereal. Press into square pan until set. Cut into bars. Variation: Drop by teaspoons onto waxed paper.

30

"C" Vocabulary and Oral Expression

Introducing "C"
Introduce "c" words through conversation, illustrations, and questions. (Have you ever seen a camel? Where? Can you describe it? What are coins? Which coin is one cent?)

Foods

cake	cupcakes
cookies	coconut
carrots	catsup
cauliflower	cabbage
cucumber	cranberries
corn	cocoa
cream	custard

Names

Calvin	Clara
Carl	Carla
Clarence	Carol
Clifford	Cassie
Corey	Colleen
Craig	Connie
Curtis	Christine
Candy	Cathy

Animals

cow
camel
cat
crow
caterpillar
crocodile
crab
cricket

"C" Sounds
C, at times, makes the "s" sound, as in the following words:

city	center	cinnamon
cent	circus	cider
Cindy	circle	cereal
celery	ceiling	

You may wish to teach your children that C makes the "s" sound when followed by e, i, or y.

"C" Objects

Ask, "Can you tell me about any of the following things?" (Make a note of those things that no one can describe and provide pictures at a later date.)

cabin	camera	canteen	catalog
clover	caboose	candle	couch
cape	collar	cage	cork
canoe	cartoon	compass	costume

Tongue Twisters

- Ask children to repeat in unison after you. Then ask if anyone would like to try to say a tongue twister as fast as possible alone.

Corey can carry Carl's coat.   *Carla cleans closets.*
Connie colors and cuts cloth.   *Calico cat caught Calvin.*
Cindy sips cinnamon cider. (soft c sound)   *Clarence clown cuts costumes.*

- Now ask the students to add one or more "c" words to the following to make tongue twisters:

Cassie cooks........
Clifford counts.......
Carl caught..........
Cliff climbs........
Carol calls.........

- Tell the children to answer "yes" or "no" to these questions and to explain why they answered as they did.

Can a cab clap?   *Can you carry clothes?*
Can clippers cut?   *Can you count cash?*
Can cotton climb?   *Can a clock cook?*
Can you cover a cot?   *Does a corner curve?*

"C" Art and Activities

Use Your Senses

Sense of Touch and Smell
1. Duplicate the letter "C" on page 29.
2. Cover with glue. Sprinkle on any type of cereal bits.
3. Have students close their eyes and feel the page.
4. Repeat with cinnamon and have the students smell the page.

Sense of Taste
Have "Cookie Day." Each child brings in a few of his favorite cookies. Break the cookies into bite-size pieces for sharing. Allow each child to measure and stir a cup of instant cocoa to have with the cookies. Have a "c" tasting day. Let students try carrots, cauliflower, cucumbers, coconut, cabbage, corn, custard, or cranberries.

Sense of Hearing
Ask students to imitate and think of things that make these sounds: crash, clang, crunch, click, creak, cry.

Sense of Sight
When children are out of the room, place items beginning with the letter "c" in clear view (clock, calendar, closet, crayons, cabinet, cap, candy, coat, cat, etc.). When students return, begin a game by saying, "I spy a 'c' object in the room..." and give a clue to its identity (i.e., "...that you might wear on your head"). The student who guesses correctly may then say "I spy." An adult may need to whisper a suggestion for an object or clue.

Make a Calico Cat

Read *Hello Calico!*, by Karma Wilson (Little Simon, 2007). This is only one of a series of stories about Calico that the children may enjoy. Have each child complete a Candy-Eyed Calico Cat. You will need a copy of the pattern (page 34) for each child, glue, small scraps of patterned material, toothpicks, and flat candies (two for each cat).

Give children these directions: Apply a light layer of glue to the cat. Cover as much of the cat as possible with material scraps. Glue on toothpicks for whiskers. Glue on two flat candies for eyes.

Candy-Eyed Calico Cat Pattern

Clay Cat

Use your own clay or the recipe below. After molding the cats, students may use toothpicks for whiskers.

Clay
2 cups flour
1 cup salt
1 cup water
2 tablespoons cooking oil
few drops of food coloring (optional)

Mix the flour and salt together. Add the oil and food coloring to the water. Add this liquid to the dry ingredients a little at a time. Knead until a soft dough forms. (The above recipe makes about four cups of clay.) Tightly covered, it can be stored in a refrigerator for a few weeks. The clay cats can be air dried.

Circle and Clothespin Critters

Materials: a copy of page 36 for each student
crayons or markers
clip clothespins—two for each child
scraps of yarn, string, ribbon
glue

Duplicate the number of circle pages you will need. Direct each child to color the circles the color(s) of their choice, to cut them out, to arrange the circles to form a "critter" and to glue them together. They may glue on pieces of paper scrap for tails. Two clothespins clipped to the bottom of the body will allow the "critter" to stand. Let students name their "critters."

Circle Patterns

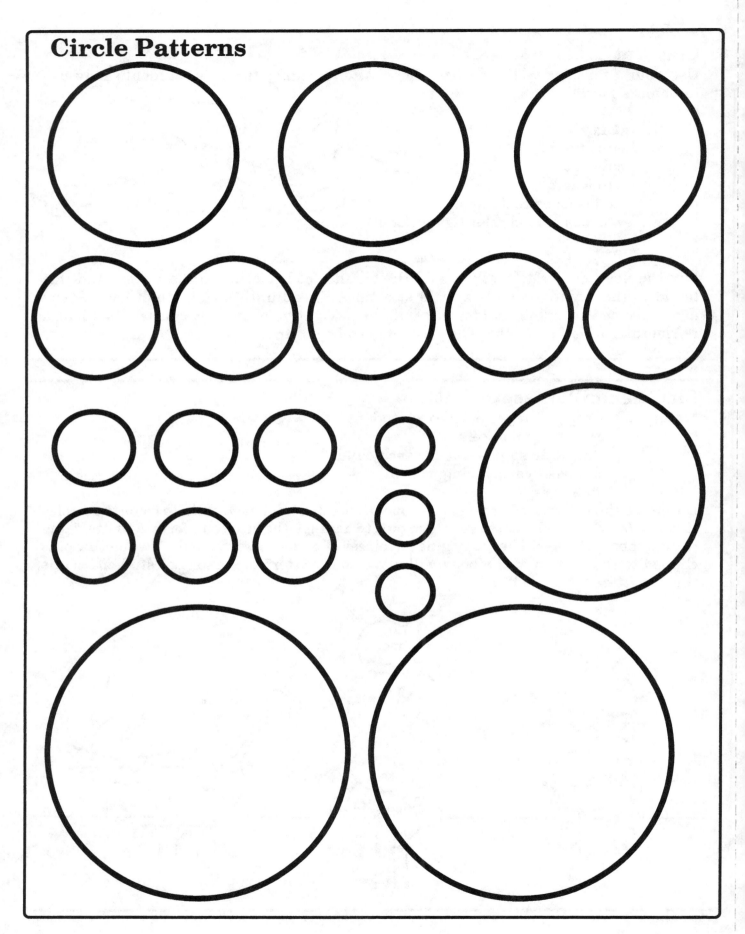

36

"C" Colors

Color Books
Read the following books about colors:
  Is It Red? Is It Yellow? Is It Blue? by Tana Hoban. Greenwillow, 1978.
  Color Kittens, by Margaret Wise Brown. Golden Books, 1958.

Looking for Colors
Play "I'm Thinking." Leader says, "I'm thinking of something in the room that is... (*names a color*)." The object should be in clear view and large enough for all the children to see. The children guess. The correct guesser becomes the leader. If no one guesses correctly after a reasonable amount of time, hints may be given.

Color Mixing
Use drops of food coloring in water and paints on paper to illustrate how:
  red and blue make purple
  red and yellow make orange
  blue and yellow make green

Ask children to work with their crayons or paint boxes and try the color combinations illustrated. Then ask them to experiment and try to make other colors. To get them started, you might ask, "How do you think we could make pink, gray, or tan?"

Color Scramble
Hide strips of the basic colors around the room. See how many different colors students can find in a minute.

Camouflage
Talk about camouflage. Why would animals want to be the same color as their background? Do people ever use camouflage? Why?

Read:
The Mixed-Up Chameleon, by Eric Carle. HarperCollins, 1988.
A Color of His Own, by Leo Lionni. Pantheon, 1976.

Camouflage Hide and Seek

You will need wooden tongue depressors or ice cream sticks. While children are out of the room, hide several tongue depressors that have been colored the same color as the background where you will lay them. When the children enter, ask them to hunt for the tongue depressors. When all have been found, talk about whether they were easy or hard to find. Then give each child a depressor and crayons. Say, "I want you to pretend you are this stick. You are an insect. Look around the room and decide where you would like to live. Color yourself so your enemies will not see you." When everyone has finished, small groups of children may take turns hiding their sticks while the others hide their eyes. When all are hidden, they "hunt" the insects. This is an excellent activity to do outside, too.

Camouflage Walk

Hide some things outdoors that are "out of place" but not easy to see because of camouflage. (Some good examples are a green toothbrush hanging in the leaves of a tree, a brown article of clothing on a tree branch, a green box in a bush and a silver pen leaning against a flag pole.) Ask the children to look for the objects.

Colored Cornmeal

It is a good idea to spread newspapers over the work area for this activity. Mix dry powdered paint with cornmeal. Have children paint a picture or design with white glue. (Small bottles with pointed tops work best.) Sprinkle the colored cornmeal over the picture and shake off the extra. Let artwork dry before displaying. (Variation: You can also use colored coconut. Place coconut in containers of food coloring and water. Allow to soak until desired color appears. Spread out on paper towels to dry. Use method above to produce art work.)

"Color, Cut, and Clip" Clothes Line Art

Ask children to color, cut out, and clip "c" objects to a clothes line stretched across the room. Pictures could also be cut from catalogs. Use clip clothespins. You might want to limit their pictures to things they would find on a clothes line.

Talk About Clocks

Read *Telling Time with Big Mama Cat*, by Dan Harper (HMH Books, 1998). Have each child make a clock using the patterns on pages 40 and 41. You will need one paper fastener for each student. Duplicate enough patterns for your class and ask them to cut out the clock numbers and hands on page 41. Then have students glue the number circles on the clock pattern (page 40) on the appropriate "x"s. Fasten the hands to the clock with a paper fastener.

Clock Pattern

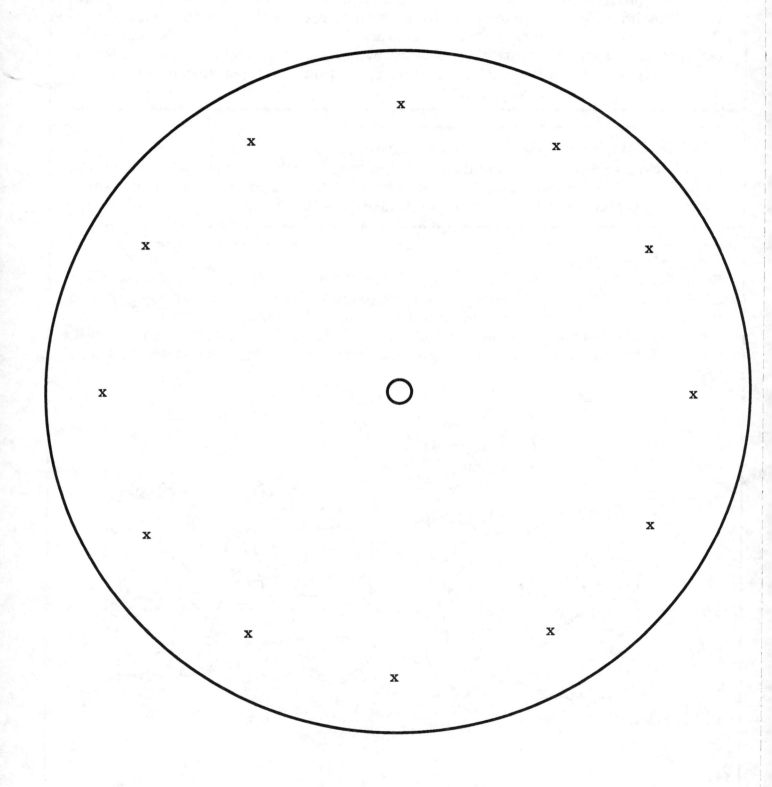

Clock Hands and Numerals

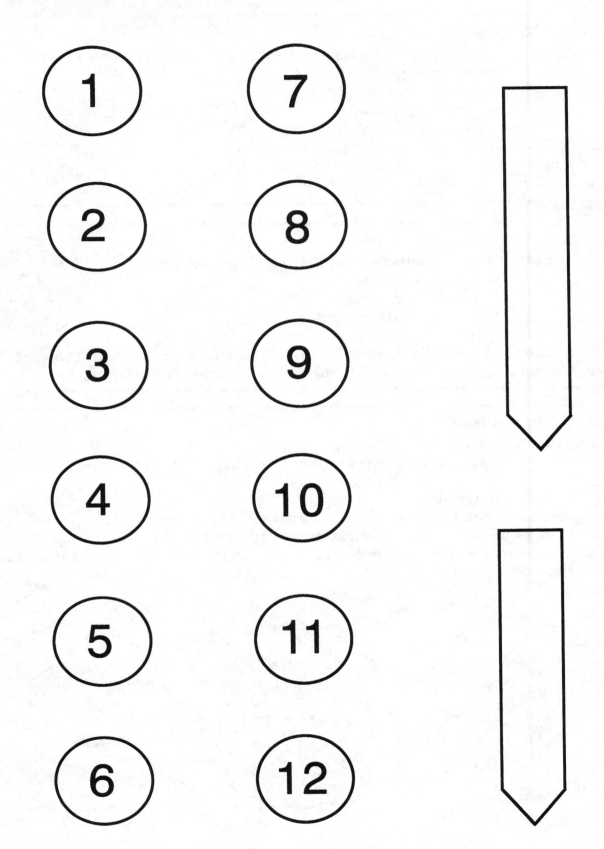

"C" Foods

Clown Cupcakes

You will need: 1 cupcake per child (purchased or prepared from a packaged mix)
paper triangles for clown hats
bowls of colored frostings
knives for spreading
various small candies, nuts, raisins

Direct each child to frost the top of a cupcake, place
the triangle at the top for the hat, and decorate the
rest to look like a clown face.

Cucumber Cats

You will need: large cucumbers cut into thick slices (one per child)
cheese spreads
knives for spreading
thin strips of carrot and celery
raisins

Direct children to spread cheese on top of each cucumber slice, add raisin eyes, ears, nose, and mouths. Have them make whiskers with carrot and celery strips.

Curly Characters

You will need: carrots, celery, radishes
bits of any other vegetables your class might eat
vegetable parer, knife
paper plates

Using the parer and knife, make carrot and celery curls, sticks, and slices. Cut thin circular slices of carrots and radishes. Have children take the cut up vegetables and arrange them on a paper plate to form a "Curly Character." They might like to name their characters. They should walk around and look at all the examples before they eat their "art."

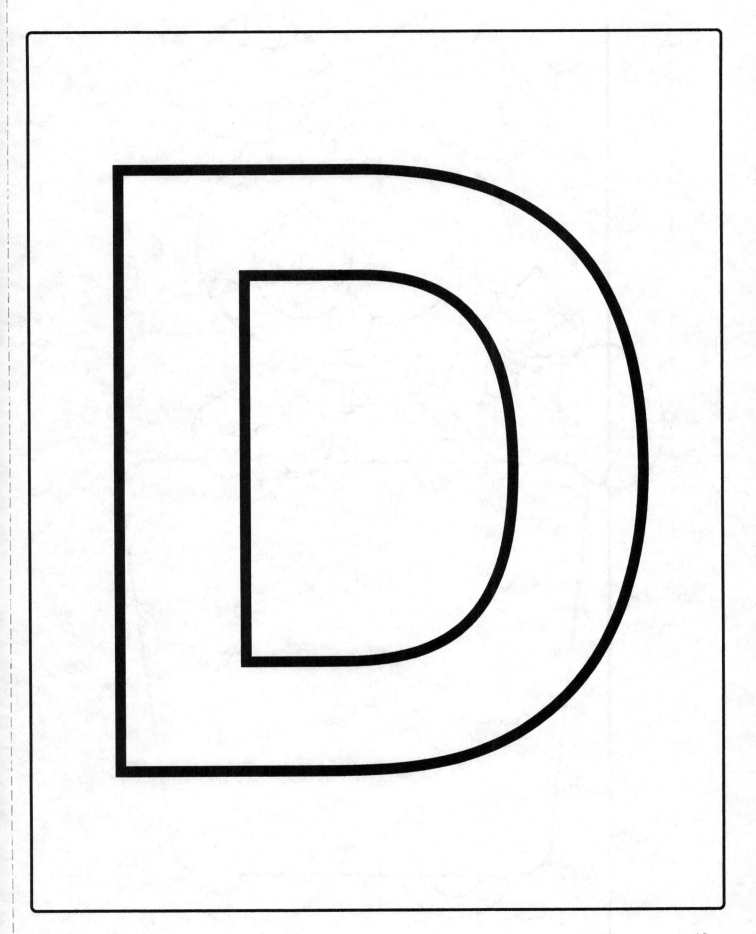

44

"D" Vocabulary and Oral Expression

Introducing "D"

Introduce "d" words through conversation, illustrations, and questions. (What time of day is dawn? Could you come to the blackboard and draw a diamond? What have you had delivered to your house?)

Names

Daisy	Diane
Dora	David
Darryl	Danny
Dan	Debbie
Donna	Denise
Darlene	Donald
Doris	Dolly
Dexter	Douglas
Dennis	
Doreen	
Dawn	
Dwayne	

Animals

deer (doe, female)
duck (drake, male)
donkey
dog
dolphin
dormouse

Careers

dancer	detective
decorator	director
delivery person	doctor
dentist	

"D" Homonyms

Ask students to tell the meaning of these "d" homonyms:

    die-dye
    doe-dough
    dew-do-due

You may also give one of the homonym meanings and ask students to spell the correct word.

"D" Opposites

Ask students to tell the opposites of these words:

day	dry	do
dirty	dark	down

You may also give other words and ask students to tell "d" words which are opposite of the words you name:

night	wet	don't
clean	light	up

"D" Objects

Ask, "Can you tell me about any of the following things?" (Make a note of those things that no one can describe and provide pictures at a later date.)

dipper	dwarf	dock
drill	dictionary	drapes
dessert	daffodil	depot
drain	dial	dairy

Tongue Twisters

- Ask children to repeat in unison after you. Then ask if anyone would like to try to say a tongue twister as fast as possible alone.

Danny is a dandy dancer.   *Donald Deacon dropped a dollar.*
Dolly dried Dora's dishes.   *The drink dribbled down Dottie's dress.*
Darrell's doghouse is dirty.   *David's daughter delivered a dozen diapers.*

- Now ask students to add one or more "d" words to the following to make tongue twisters:

  Debbie decorates..........
  Doreen draws.............
  Daisy's doll.............
  Daddy dislikes...........
  Dick drives..............
  Donna decides to ....

- Tell the children to answer "yes" or "no" to these questions and to explain why they answered as they did.

Would you drink darts?   *Is a doe a deer?*
Could a detective make a discovery?   *Is a drake a duck?*
Can a dictionary drink?   *Could a decorator dance?*
Could you draw a dipper?   *Can drapes droop?*

"D" Art and Activities

Use Your Senses

Sense of Touch and Smell
1. Duplicate the letter "D" on page 43.
2. Cover with glue. Sprinkle with fine dirt.
3. Have students close their eyes, then feel the letter.
4. Cover another letter "D" with glue and sprinkle on powdered detergent.
5. Have students smell. (You can also use dill weed and/or dry mustard.)

Sense of Taste
Let students taste dates and/or various foods that contain dates.

Sense of Hearing
Select one child to be Mr./Ms. Doorbell. Everyone else closes their eyes. The doorbell moves to different corners of the room and says, "Ding dong." With eyes still closed, children should point to the direction from which they hear the sound coming. They might also hold up a number of fingers indicating how many times they heard the doorbell ring.

Sense of Sight
Discuss the meaning of the words dim and dark. If possible, demonstrate in your room. Play "I Spy." When children are out of the room, place items beginning with the letter "d" in clear view (such as a doll, a duck, or dishes). When students return, begin a game by saying, "I spy a 'd' object in the room..." and give a clue to its identity (i.e., "...that you might see in a pond"). The student who guesses correctly may then say "I spy." An adult may need to whisper a suggestion for an object or clue.

What Will Dissolve?
Prepare a table with cups of water, spoons, and various substances (some that will dissolve and some that will not). Discuss and demonstrate what the word dissolve means. Then ask the children which things they think will dissolve and which will not. Let them experiment on their own and report their findings. On the table, you might have salt, sugar, baking powder, sand, dry gelatin, powdered drink mix, marbles, dice, etc.

Diary Days
Discuss the meaning of the word diary. Keep a class diary for a week with entries dictated to you by the children. Print on a large chart for all to see and reread each day.

Dinosaur Match

Duplicate the dinosaurs on pages 49 and 50 so that you and each child have copies. Direct the children to color and cut out the dinosaurs. When all are finished, play dinosaur match. Hold up one of your dinosaurs and describe it using the information below or any other reference material you wish. Ask each child to find his dinosaur that matches yours and place it on his desk. (Toilet paper tubes can be taped to the backs to make the dinosaurs stand upright.) When all dinosaurs have been identified, allow time to use them in free play.

For your reference:

Apatosaurus (uh-pat-o-sawr-us) This dinosaur was once known as brontosaurus. It was one of the largest, about 80 feet long. Though huge, the only thing it had for self defense was its long tail. Can you find this dinosaur?

Compsognathus (komp-sug-nay-thus) With a length of only a foot and a half, this was one of the smallest dinosaurs. It had strong back legs and could run very fast. It had short front legs which ended with feet with three large claws. Do you see a dinosaur that looks like that?

Stegosaurus (steg-o-sawr-us) It had sharp spikes on its tail and a row of bony plates on its back that looked like triangles. It had a very small head and brain. Find your stegosaurus.

Triceratops (try-sair-a-tops) It had three enormous horns pointing forward. They looked like spears. It probably used these to defend itself. Look for these three horns and hold up your Triceratops.

Tyrannosaurus (tie-ran-o-sawr-us) It was the biggest meat-eating animal that ever lived. Often called "Tyrannosaurus Rex," which means "king of the dinosaurs." Do you think you know which one he is?

Dinosaur Patterns

Dinosaur Patterns

Dirt Drawings

You will need: dishes of loose dirt
bowl
plastic silverware
construction paper
white glue
crayons or markers

Very loose dirt that does not have a lot of moisture in it will work best for this activity. Have several bowls of dirt within easy reach of the children. Ask them to draw pictures or designs on their paper with white glue. (Glue containers with pointed tips work best.) Students can use the plastic silverware to sprinkle the dirt on the glue. They can shake the extra dirt from the paper, then add detail to the pictures with crayons or markers. Allow glue to dry before displaying.

Dot Pictures

For this activity, use paper confetti or collect a large number of punch outs from a paper punch. (Children might help gather these a few days before the activity.) Have children draw pictures and glue on dots where they wish or simply do dot designs. Some may wish to make their dots form a diamond or a "D."

Design a Drum

You will need: empty coffee cans
all sizes of extra plastic lids
white contact paper
crayons
markers
glue
pencils
spools or sticks (for drumsticks)

Cut the bottom off of each can and cover both ends with a plastic lid. Cover the curved surface with white contact paper. Have the children decorate their cans with crayons and markers. Glue the sharpened end of a pencil into a spool for a drumstick. (Any wooden stick or unsharpened pencil could also be used.)

"D" Games

Doggie, Doggie, Where Is Your Bone?

The players sit in a circle with a chair in the center. A bone is placed under the chair. (This could be a rubber bone or a paper one.) The player chosen to be the doggie sits in the chair and covers his eyes with his hands. Another player sneaks up and takes the bone, sits down, and hides it behind his back. Everyone says, "Doggie, Doggie, where is your bone?" Doggie gets three guesses. If he guesses correctly, the doggie takes a seat in the circle and the player who stole the bone becomes the new doggie. After three turns, if he has not guessed correctly, a new doggie is selected.

Dominoes

You will need: one copy of page 53 per child
one envelope per child
scissors
pair(s) of dice

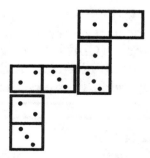

Have children cut out all of their dominoes and place them in an envelope. Explain that two children will play together and will only need to use one set of dominoes. Pair up the children and give them the following directions: Find the domino that has one dot on each end, and place it face up between you. Turn all the remaining dominoes over so that you cannot see the dots. Each player draws five and turns them face up in front of him. The remaining dominoes are the "boneyard." Each player rolls the dice and the one who rolls the biggest number goes first. He tries to match up one of his dominoes with the one in the center. (It must have one dot on one end.) If he cannot, he takes a domino from the "boneyard," and it is player two's turn. The first one to have no dominoes in front of him is the winner. Less mature children can use their dominoes for counting and matching activities.

52

Domino Patterns

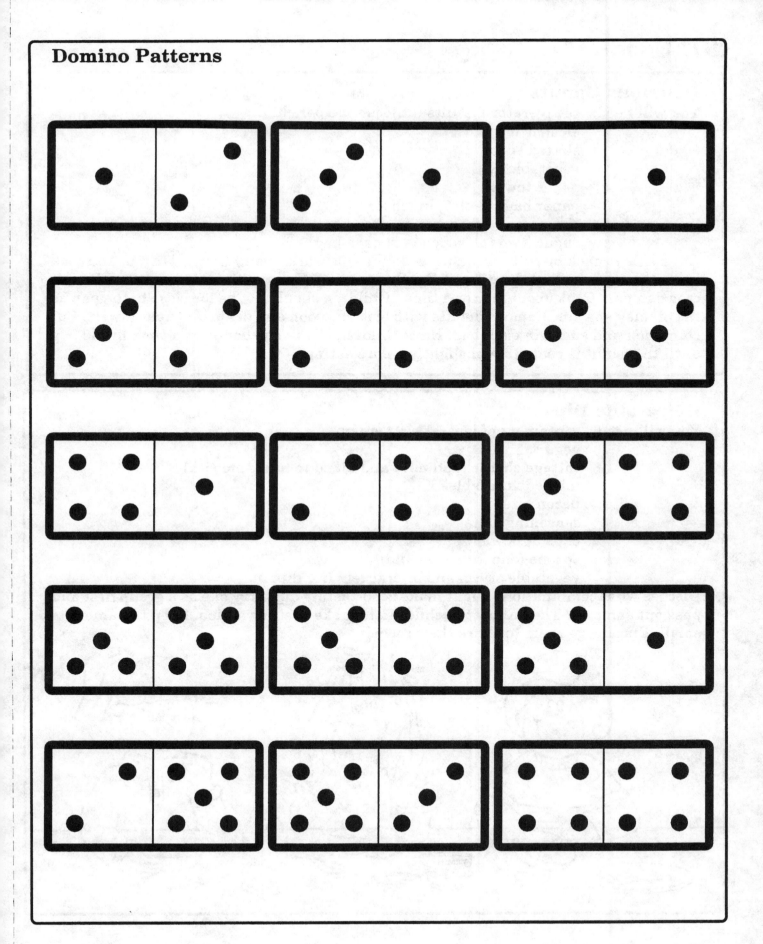

"D" Foods

Delicious Donuts

You will need: refrigerator biscuits (at least one per child)
electric fry pan
slotted spoon
vegetable oil
paper towels
paper bags (4 or 5, lunch size)
cinnamon (a teaspoon in each bag)
sugar (two tablespoons in each bag)

Cut a hole in each biscuit center. (A clean thimble works well.) Heat oil in pan and cook biscuit donuts on high heat until lightly browned. Turn with slotted spoon. (Do not crowd in pan. Cook about four at a time.) Children should not be too close to the pan as the oil may spatter. Remove donuts with slotted spoon and drain on paper towels. Put cinnamon and sugar in each bag. Have children shake one donut at a time in the bag until the donut is coated. Cool slightly before eating.

Delectable Dips

You will need: containers of low-fat sour cream
yogurt
cottage cheese (add milk and blend to make smooth)
minced vegetables
bacon bits
seasoning salts
cups or bowls
spoons (one for each child)
vegetable sticks and/or crackers (for dipping)

Discuss what combinations might make good-tasting dips. Try one as a group first and pass out samples. Then allow the children to make their own dips. Keep the amounts small. Encourage them to share their recipes.

54

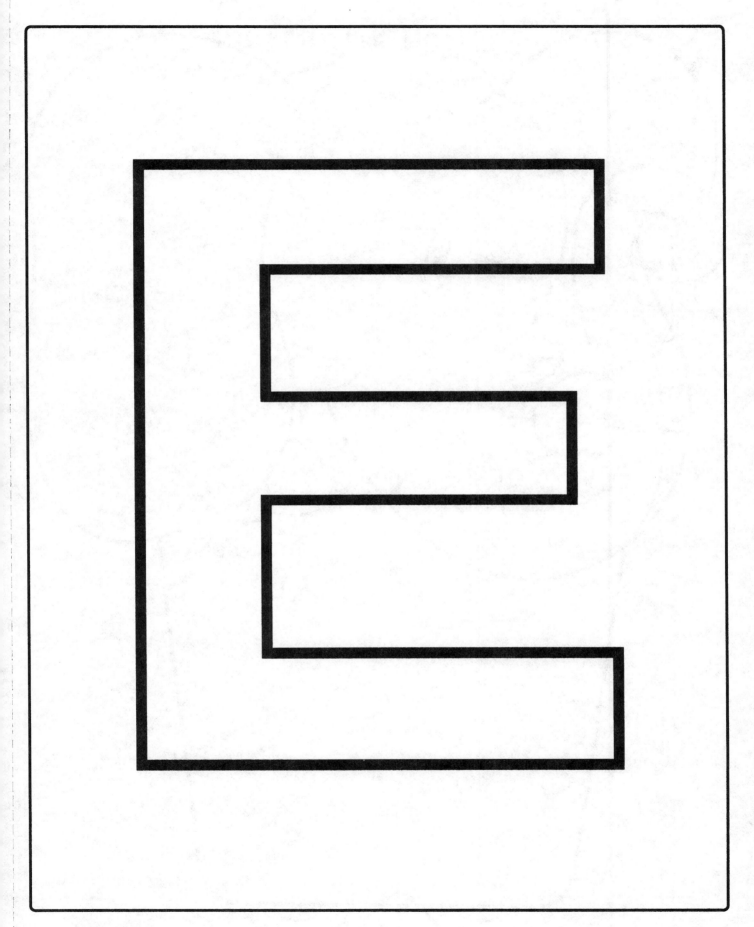

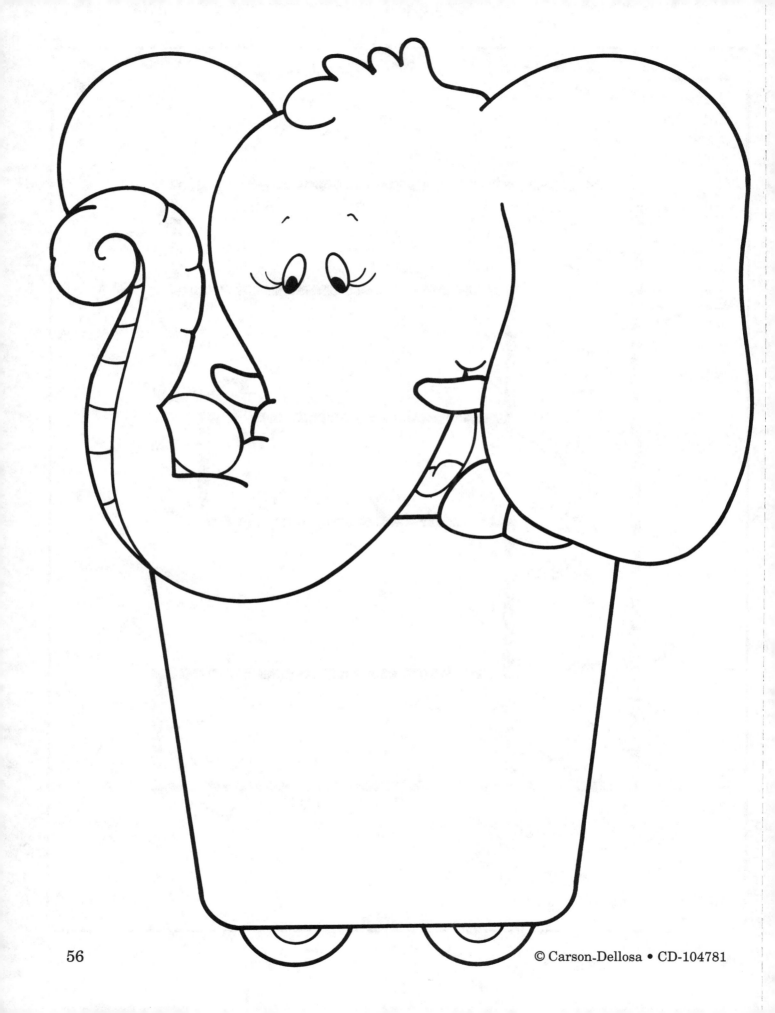

56

"E" Vocabulary and Oral Expression

Introducing "E"

Introduce "e" words through conversation, illustrations, and questions. (What things do you use that run by electricity? Do you have any elastic in your clothing? If your mother says she is going to entertain friends, what does that mean?)

Names

Elizabeth	Ernie
Eleanor	Eileen
Elmer	Elise
Ella	Ellen
Elaine	Elsie
Emily	Emma
Erica	Esther
Eve	Evelyn
Earl	Edward
Edwin	Elliot
Eric	Erwin
Evan	Ethan

Opposites
- east—west
- early—late
- empty—full
- end—beginning
- evening—morning
- enormous—small
- easy—hard

Animals
- eagle
- eel
- elephant
- elk
- egret

"E" Actions

Ask, "What things do you know that can do these things?"

escape	evaporate
erase	eat
echo	exit

"E" Objects

Ask, "Can you tell me about any of the following things?" (Make a note of those that no one can describe and provide pictures at a later date.)

earmuffs	earphones	easel
engine	elevator	eraser
Eskimo	envelope	escalator
earth	elk	eyelash

Tongue Twisters

- Ask children to repeat in unison after you. Then ask if anyone would like to try to say a tongue twister as fast as possible alone.

  Elmer Elephant has enormous ears. *Ernie eel enjoys exercising.*
  Ella Eagle laid eleven eggs. *Ernie easily erases errors.*
  Elsie eats eight eggs. *Every evening Eric Elk escapes.*

- Ask the children if they can add one or more "e" words to the following to make tongue twisters.

  Elsie Egret entertains... *Edwin Edwards enjoys...*
  Ella Elf eats... *Earl has eight...*
  Eighty Eskimos... *Each evening Elizabeth...*

- Tell the children to answer "yes" or "no" to these questions and to explain why they answered as they did.

  Can an envelope be empty? *Are earmuffs electric?*
  Is eleven more than eight? *Can you hear an echo?*
  Is an easel elastic? *Is an evergreen a type of tree?*
  Would an elevator eat eggplant? *Are some elephants enormous?*

"E" Art and Activities

Use Your Senses

Senses of Touch and Smell:
1. Duplicate the letter "e" on page 55.
2. Cover it with glue. Sprinkle with crushed eggshells.
3. Have students close their eyes, then feel the page.
4. Repeat using needles from an evergreen tree. Have students smell.

Sense of Taste

Prepare eggs in different ways. Children might enjoy tasting poached, hard-boiled, or deviled eggs.

Sense of Hearing

Ask students to "echo" your words. This activity may also be done in pairs. One child can be the voice and the other can be the echo, and then they can switch.

Sense of Sight

When children are out of the room, place items beginning with the letter "e" in clear view (eraser, easel, elephant, envelopes, etc.). When students return, begin a game by saying, "I spy an 'e' object in the room..." and give a clue to its identity (i.e., "...that you might use to fix a mistake"). The student who guesses correctly may then say "I spy." An adult may need to whisper a suggestion for an object or clue.

Egg People

You will need: hard-boiled eggs
a copy of page 60 for each child
yarn or scrap materials
markers

Tell the children to color the egg stand from the pattern page any way they wish. Cut out and tape or glue as shown above the pattern. Color two eyes and two ears from the pattern page for each egg person. Cut out the colored eyes and ears, fold on the dotted lines and glue to the egg. Glue on yarn for hair and use scrap materials and markers to add additional decorations, facial features, etc.

Egg People Patterns

sample

fold | fold

fold | fold

fold | fold

front | back — tape

Electricity

- Look for clues that things around the room run by electricity (switches, outlets, cords, bulbs, pull chains).
- Talk about the following electricity-related topics:

    safety (with outlets, around water, stove, iron, etc.)

    conserving energy Select an electricity monitor each day to turn out lights when not needed (classroom and restroom) and to make sure recorders, etc., are not left running.

    a day without electricity Most children have experienced being without electricity for a short time. Ask them to think about what it would be like if the power was out for an entire day.

- Go for an electricity walk around your building. Look for clues of things that use electricity. Find out if any lights stay on during a power shortage (such as exit lights). Walk outside if you have a traffic light or if there are other lights in use nearby.

"Eat" the Alphabet

A good reference for this activity is *Eating the Alphabet: Fruits and Vegetables from A to Z*, by Lois Ehlert (Harcourt Brace Jovanovich, 1989). An excellent section at the end gives a picture of each food mentioned and resource information about it. Assign each child a letter. If a child cannot think of a food to match his letter, give suggestions and/or pictures. Have him draw the item, cut out two copies to match together front to back, and color both. Show students how to staple the edges of the two cutouts leaving an opening and stuff the object with scrap cloth or paper. The openings may then be stapled shut and all foods can be put on the bulletin board for display.

Egg Carton Art

You will need:
       egg cartons
       scissors
       markers or paint
       pipe cleaners
       colored paper

Remove the lid from the carton and cut the bottom in half lengthwise. This will give you two strips of egg cups that can be used as the bodies of interesting insects and "critters." Pipe cleaners, markers, and colored paper can be used to add body parts.

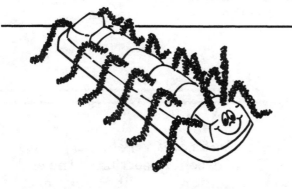
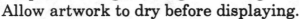

Egg Shell Art

You will need:
       crushed egg shells
       food coloring
       glue
       construction paper

You will need a large amount of crushed egg shells for this activity. Sending a note home to parents asking for leftover shells will help. Soak egg shells in a solution of food coloring and water. Prepare a number of different colors. When shells are the color you desire, remove and spread on paper towels to dry. Direct children to make a large, simple drawing or design and to glue on the crushed egg shells wherever they wish. Allow artwork to dry before displaying.

62

"E" Food

Super Scrambled Eggs

You will need:
a copy of the book *Scrambled Eggs Super!* by Dr. Seuss. Random House, 1953.

an appropriate number of eggs so each child can have a taste

ingredients to add to eggs (cheese, parsley, bits of vegetables and meat, seasonings, etc.)

non-stick fry pan

hot plate or stove

spatula

bowl

spoon

plates

forks

If you wish, you can decorate the shells of the eggs that will be used and introduce them as Dr. Seuss presents each "different" egg.

- Read *Scrambled Eggs Super!*
- Make scrambled eggs. Give every child a turn doing something, such as cracking an egg, stirring, or adding an ingredient. An adult should do the cooking. Then give each child a taste of the "Super Scrambled Eggs."
- **Optional Activity** Read *Green Eggs and Ham,* by Dr. Seuss (Random House, 1960). Color a small portion of your scrambled eggs green using food coloring. Then, just like Sam-I-Am who tries to get his friend to try something new, see how many children will taste the green eggs. Ask them if they taste different.

64

"F" Vocabulary and Oral Expression

Introducing "F"

Introduce "f" words through conversation, illustrations, and questions. Can anyone write the numeral five on the blackboard? (four, fourteen, fifteen, any numerals between forty and fifty-nine) If you made a frame, how could you use it?

Names		Homonyms	Animals
Fred	Faith	fur-fir	fox
Frank	Faye	for-four	falcon
Florence	Freda	fair-fare	frog
Fanny	Fritz	fairy-ferry	flamingo
Felix	Farley	flour-flower	fish
Frances	Fern	flew-flu	
		feet-feat	

"F" Actions

Ask, "What things do you know that can do the following things?"

fade	faint	fight	fly
freeze	flash	flip	frown

What things do you know that are fast? funny? flat? fancy?

"F" Objects

Ask, "Can you tell me about any of the following things?" (Make a note of those that no one can describe and provide pictures at a later date.)

factory	faucet	fence	Ferris wheel
filter	forehead	football	flame
fiddle	flood	field	film

Tongue Twisters

- Ask children to repeat in unison after you. Then ask if anyone would like to try to say a tongue twister as fast as possible alone.

  Frank Farmer felt funny.   *The fall flies flew.*
  Florence found forty fleas.   *Fred falcon flew forward.*
  Faith's father found five feathers.   *Fanny's favorite fruit froze.*
  Faye's fancy fabric faded.   *Freddy's friend fixed Farley's faucet.*

- Ask the children if they can add one or more "f" words to the following to make tongue twisters:

  Fern's family found...
  A friendly fellow followed...
  Flo Floyd forgot...
  The famous flamingo frightened...
  Frankie fixed french fries for...
  Foster's father...

- Tell the children to answer "yes" or "no" to these questions and to explain why they answered as they did.

  Can fabric fade?   *Can you follow a friend?*
  Can a floor forget?   *Do fathers have foreheads?*
  Can you feed a factory?   *Could a farmer give a feast?*
  Can you put foil on food? *Would you put frosting on a football?*

"F" Art and Activities

What Will Float?

Have a large group of objects—some which will float, others that will not—around a water table or large tub of water. Ask the children to guess if each object will float or sink. Then let them test to see. Allow free time to let them "sail" objects and to experiment on their own.

Use Your Senses

Sense of Touch

1. Duplicate the letter "F" on page 64.
2. Cover with glue. Lay on fur, feathers or felt.
3. Have students close their eyes and then feel the page.

Sense of Smell

Have children close their eyes or blindfold them. See if each one can identify a fruit scent. Use scented stickers or markers, candies, or cut real fruit to release the odor.

Sense of Hearing

Tell children to close their eyes. Say "f" words to them faintly. Ask them to raise their hands if they can repeat the word. Keep moving away and getting fainter and fainter until no one can hear what you say.

Sense of Taste

Let students discuss and taste some favorite flavors (vanilla, chocolate, strawberry). Provide a fig or something that contains figs (such as cookies) for them to taste.

Sense of Sight

When children are out of the room, place items beginning with the letter "f" in clear view (fan, faucet, fern, file cabinet, floor, the numerals 4 and 5, etc.). When students return, begin a game by saying, "I spy an 'f' object in the room..." and give a clue to its identity (i.e., "...that you might use to blow air"). The student who guesses correctly may then say "I spy." An adult may need to whisper a suggestion for an object or clue.

Finger Painting

You will need:
      liquid laundry starch
      paint or food coloring
      glossy paper
      old shirts or smocks
      newspaper

Before starting this activity, cover the work area with newspapers and the painters with smocks. Mix the paint or food coloring with the laundry starch. Wet the paper and spoon on several teaspoons of the starch fingerpaint. You may use one or several colors. Instruct the children to swirl the paint around with sweeping motions, blending the colors and changing the design as many times as they wish. Set aside to dry.

Variation: Whip up soap flakes and add food coloring.

Face Painting

You will need:
      1 tablespoon solid shortening
      2 tablespoons cornstarch
      food coloring

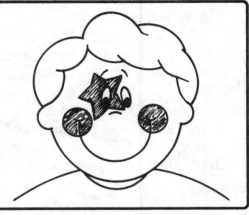

The above ingredients can be mixed together and stored in an airtight container. This face paint is non-toxic and washes off with soap and water. If children are going to do their own face painting, they should wear something to cover their clothes and mirrors should be available.

Funny Faces

Ask each child to draw one large oval on his paper. Then have each one cut out facial features from old magazines (such as eyes, ears, mouth, and nose) and glue them on the oval. Students can use yarn and glue to add hair and then they can name their "Funny Faces."

Foil Art

Have students mold lightweight foil into shapes. Encourage them to try some "f" shapes (fish, feet, frog, fork, the numerals 4 and 5).

Flour Fingerpainting

Sprinkle (or let someone sift) flour onto dark paper. Allow the students time to explore making different pictures and designs. Suggest that they trace their hands, practice specific shapes, draw "f" objects and/or the letter F. Have students finish with their favorite flour fingerpaintings. Give children time to walk around and view what others have done. After this activity, the flour can be dumped into a container and used again.

Fingerprints

Use an ink pad and let children make their own fingerprints. Discuss how they are different and how they are alike. Children will be interested to learn how fingerprints are used to identify people.

Fancy Fuzzies

You will need: 1 copy of the patterns on page 71
yarn scraps, old sweaters, socks that can be cut up, fuzzy fabric
materials for decorating (buttons, beads, trim, ribbon, etc.)
glue
scissors

A letter home to parents asking for scrap materials will help build your supply for this activity. Tell the children to cut out one or more patterns from page 71. Glue the fuzzy material to the pattern and then decorate to make a fancy or funny fuzzie.

70

Fancy Fuzzies Patterns

"F" Games

Freeze
Play music and tell the children to move or dance while they listen. Stop the music periodically and say, "Freeze." Children should try to remain in their "frozen" positions for thirty seconds. Then say, "Melt" and start the music again.

Go Fishing
You will need: one copy of the fish patterns (page 73) per child
a fishing pole (long stick, branch, yardstick)
magnet
string
paper clips
crayons
scissors

Tie the magnet to one end of the piece of string and attach the other end to the "fishing pole." Tell the children to color and cut out one or more of the fish on page 73. Attach a paper clip to each fish. Put all the fish in a large container (bucket, dish pan). See how many fish (let them count) each child can catch in a given amount of time.

Fish Patterns

"F" Food

Fruit Juice Freezie Pops

Put fruit juice in paper cups and partially freeze. Insert ice cream sticks and freeze until firm. Cut off paper cup.

Variation: Freeze fruit juice in ice cube trays and insert an ice cream stick.

Frosted Funny-Faced Cookies

This activity requires large, flat, round cookies and frosting. The cookies may be bought, made at home, or made at school. Bring in dull knives for spreading and varieties of candies and pointed frosting tubes for creating facial features. Tell the children to frost their cookies and create funny faces.

Fresh Fruit Kabobs

You will need wooden skewers or long picks of some type. Cut up fruits into sizes that will easily slip on the skewer. Be sure the fruit is a consistency that will not fall apart when handled. Tell the children that you will name a letter of the alphabet and they should look on the table for a fruit whose name begins with that letter. (Use only letters that have corresponding fruits.) When the kabobs are full, check to see that everyone has completed the correct pattern. Let them slide the fruits off with their fingers or forks onto a plate and enjoy.

You might select: A—apple, apricot
B—banana
C—cantaloupe
P—pineapple
O—orange
W—watermelon

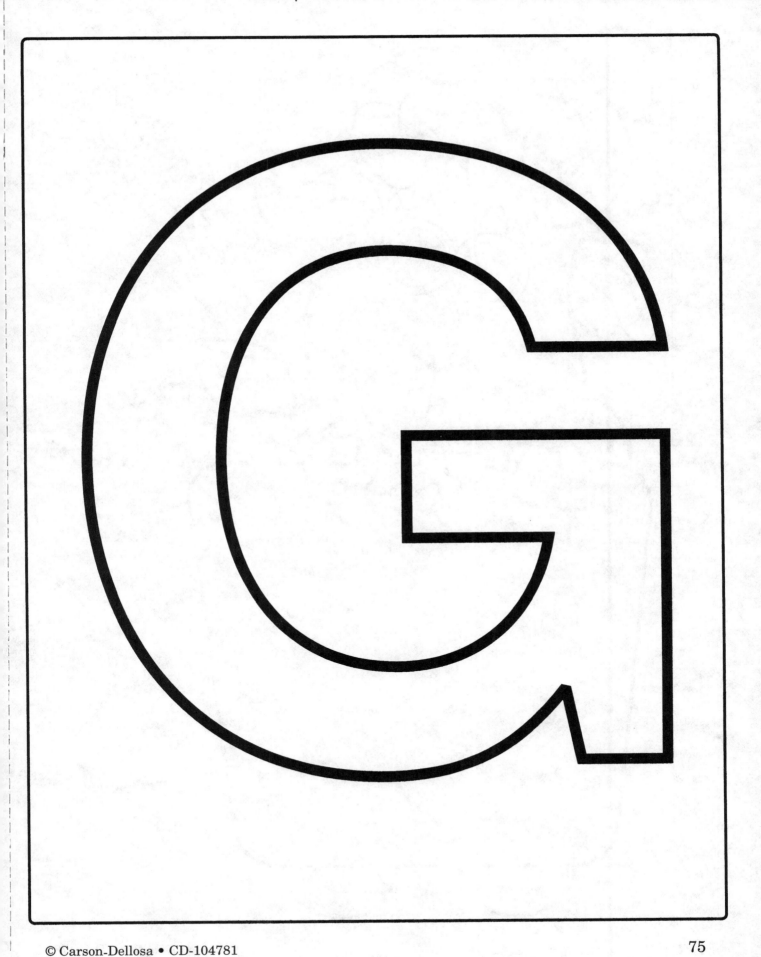

"G" Vocabulary and Oral Expression

Introducing "G"

Introduce "g" words through conversation, illustrations, and questions. (Can you make a sound like a growl? If your father's car is low on gas, what does he need to do? If your sister is in first grade, what will her grade be next year?)

Names		Foods	Animals
Gloria	Gordon	grapefruit	goose (gander, gosling)
Grace	Gail	gooseberries	gazelle
Glenn	Gwen	gravy	gibbon
Gavin	Gary	grapes	goldfish
Gus	Greg	graham crackers	gopher
Guy	Gladys	grains	gorilla
			goat

"G" Sounds

G can make the "j" sound, as in the following words:

ginger	gigantic	gentle	generous
giant	gem	giraffe	gentleman
gerbil	general	genius	gingerbread
geranium	gymnasium	ginger ale	

You may wish to teach your students that g makes the "j" sound most often when it is followed by e, i, or y.

"G" Objects

Ask, "Can you tell me about any of the following things?" (Make a note of those things that no one can describe and provide pictures at a later date.)

gallon	garden	gardenia	gate
gift	glider	globe	glove
gum	grill	gutter	goat

What things do you know that can do the following things?

gallop	giggle	glide	glisten
glow	grow	growl	glitter

Tongue Twisters

- Ask children to repeat in unison after you. Then ask if anyone would like to try to say a tongue twister as fast as possible alone.

Gordon gave Gloria a great gift.   *Gary Goat grabbed Greta's gloves.*
Goose and gander grazed on grass.   *Granny and Gracie giggled and grinned.*
Gus Grey gathers good grapes.   *Giant George is a generous gentleman.*

- Now ask the students to add one or more "g" words to the following to make tongue twisters.

  Gracie got...
  Grits and gravy are...
  Guy Goldfish greets...
  Gregory Grizzly...
  "Good-bye," said Gavin...
  Gloria Green grows...

- Tell the children to answer "yes" or "no" to these questions and to explain why they answered as they did.

  Do you grip a golf club?   *Can gravel graduate?*
  Can a girl's gown glitter?   *Can gum get gooey?*
  Could gourds grow in a garden?   *Could a girl gargle?*
  Can a gutter gallop?   *Could a guard be a guy?*

"G" Art and Activities

Use Your Senses

Sense of Touch and Smell
1. Duplicate the letter "G" on page 75.
2. Cover with glue. Sprinkle on newly cut grass.
3. Have students close their eyes and feel and smell the page.

Repeat with garlic salt or ginger and have the students smell the page.

Sense of Taste
Have a "G" tasting day. Try different grains (cereals are a good source), grapefruit (sweetened), two types of grapes, and ginger ale.

Sense of Hearing
Listen to recordings of guitar music or invite someone in to play the guitar. Tell a ghost story and assign children to make the sound effects.

Sense of Sight
Play, "I Spy." When children are out of the room, place items beginning with the letter "g" in clear view (glue, globe, goldfish, etc.). When students return, begin a game by saying, "I spy a 'g' object in the room..." and giving a clue to its identity (i.e., "that looks like a round map"). The student who guesses correctly may then say "I spy." An adult may need to whisper a suggestion for an object or clue.

Guessing Table
Set up materials on a table so you can ask the children these types of questions. Let everyone guess. "Look at this walnut. How many walnuts do you think will fit in this cup?" "Which of these three bowls will hold the water in this pitcher?" "How many jellybeans are in this jar?" "How many of these toothpicks would you need to make an end to end toothpick line across this table?" Give "Good Guesser" awards.

Green Day

Send notes home to parents to help children remember to wear green. Have a few green clothing items on hand for those who have none.

Read *Green Eggs and Ham* by Dr. Seuss (Random House Books for Young Readers, (1960).

Snack on green beans, grapes, peppers, cabbage, lettuce, etc.

Play "I Spy" using green things in your room (plants, crayons, paints, etc.).

Walk outside counting the green things you see (leaves, grass, stems, etc.).

Draw some of the green things you saw when you return to the classroom.

Mix blue and yellow paints or food colorings to make green.

Visit a greenhouse or invite a gardener to come to the classroom to discuss keeping plants healthy and green.

Gray Day

Ask children to wear or bring something in that is gray.

Read *Gray Everywhere* by Kristin Sterling (Lerner Classroom, 2010).

Paint different shades of gray using black and white paint. Paint pictures of gray objects (elephant, kitten, squirrel, goat, rain clouds, etc.). Paint pictures of objects that begin with the letter "g" (gloves, glasses, ghosts, gate, etc.).

Walk with students on "gray walk." Have them count the number of things they see that are gray.

Gumdrop Guys and Girls

GOOEY GUMMY GOOBERS

You will need toothpicks and gumdops of all sizes. Tell the children to connect the gumdrops with the toothpicks to make their characters. You can demonstrate and have one completed for them to see. When finished, let the children work in pairs or small groups making up gumdrop stories about their characters. You might give them a few titles to get them started: "Mr. and Mrs. Gumdrop's Gooey Day," "Guy and Gloria Play Games," and "Why the Gumdrops Were Grouches." Some may want to share their stories with the class. Everyone will probably want to eat the actors after they are finished. This activity could also include goats, goldfish, giraffes, and gorillas.

Goofy Goggles (Glasses)

For each pair you will need: Two connected sections of an egg carton
two pipe cleaners
paint
scrap materials (beads, yarn, etc.)

Cut out the centers of the egg carton sections. Punch one hole in each side and attach a pipe cleaner. Bend and adjust the other end of the pipe cleaner to fit over the child's ear. Let children paint and decorate as they wish.

Ghosts

Let children design their own ghosts to act out the story or for free play. Here are three suggestions:

Tissue Ghost **Lollipop Ghost** **Marshmallow Ghost**

"G" Games

Giant Steps

Establish start and finish lines using string lines or chalk. Make up steps or teach children some of the following:

    baby steps—heel to toe

    giant steps—biggest step child can make

    hop—on right foot, left foot, both feet together

    twirl—turn the body completely around for one step

    backwards steps—step toward leader backside first

    leaps—feet may leave the floor

The leader can be an adult or a mature child. All the players spread across the start line. The leader gives a command to one child at a time, saying the child's name first. "Carol, you may take two giant steps." Carol must then say, "May I?" If she forgets, she may not take the steps. If she does, the leader may answer, "Yes you may," or "No you may not." The leader may give a second command to which the player must ask, "May I?" The game goes on until one child reaches the finish line.

Gossip

Players sit in a circle. The leader whispers one or two "G" words to the person on his right (gigantic grasshoppers, greedy goats, gooey graham crackers, etc.). Each person whispers to the next until the "gossip" arrives back to the leader, who repeats what was whispered to him and then tells what he originally said. Usually the two are very different.

Guess Who

Tape a picture of a common animal on the back of each child. The children ask each other questions about themselves. When they figure out what animal they are, they can wear the picture on the front.

82

"G" game

To play the "G" Game, you will need a copy of the gameboard on page 84 for each child, colored pencils, dice and markers (pennies or buttons).

Tell the children to color in the letters on their gameboards with colored pencils. (Very sharp crayons would also work.) As they color they should think of things with names that begin with each letter. Then children can pair up and play the game, taking turns using each person's gameboard.

Directions for Play: Each player throws a die and the child with the biggest number goes first. Player one rolls the die again and moves his marker the number of spaces shown on the die. Player one must then name the letter where his marker has landed and the name of something that begins with that letter. If player two agrees, player one may stay there. If not, he must go back to the space he occupied at the beginning of the turn. (If there is a difference of opinion, an adult should be consulted.) Player two then rolls and takes his turn. The game continues until someone reaches the end. When finished, both players could get a graham cracker for playing a **good** game.

"G" Gameboard Pattern

START	F	M	R	T	A
					V
E	B	G	L		N
U			C		H
D		P	K		Q
J					W
O	X	I	S	Y	Z

"G" Foods

Granola

You will need: six cups dry oatmeal
½ cup oil
one cup honey
one cup brown sugar
two teaspoons vanilla
one cup of any of the following things:
      sunflower seeds, wheat germ
      raisins, nuts, sesame seeds, coconut

Place the oatmeal in a 9 x 13 inch pan (or the largest your toaster oven will accommodate) and toast for 10 minutes at 350°. Combine the oil, honey, sugar, and vanilla and add this mixture plus any of the other ingredients you wish to the toasted oatmeal. Bake at the same temperature 20–30 minutes. Stir two or three times while cooking. Cool.

Gingerbread Boys and Girls

Read aloud *The Gingerbread Boy*, by Paul Galdone (Houghton Mifflin, 1983). For variety read *The Gingerbread Rabbit*, by Randall Jarrell (Macmillan, 1964).

Use your favorite recipe for gingerbread cookies or, for a shortcut, use prepared gingerbread mix and the directions for making cookies on the back of the box. If you do not have a gingerbread boy cookie cutter, the children can cut out a pattern from page 86, lay it on the rolled dough, and cut around the pattern with a dull knife. The pattern can also be colored, cut out, and used to act out the story or for free play. Be sure to have frosting, raisins, and candies for decorating the gingerbread boys and girls before they "run away."

"G" Gingerbread Boy and Girl Patterns

88

"H" Vocabulary and Oral Expression

Introducing "H"

Introduce "h" words through conversation, illustrations, and questions. (If someone says, "Halt" to you, what do they want you to do? How is a hotel different from a hospital? Did you ever go on a hike? Where?)

Names		Foods	Animals
Harry	Henry	ham	hamster
Harriet	Harvey	hamburger	horse
Hal	Hilda	hash	hyena
Holly	Hope	honey	hawk
Harold	Heather	hot dogs	hedgehog
Helen	Howard		hippopotamus
			hog
			heron
			hummingbird

"H" Homonyms

Ask students to tell the meanings of these "h" homonyms:

hair-hare	hall-haul
hear-here	heard-herd
high-hi	heal-heel

"H" Opposites

Ask students to tell the opposites of these words:

hot	healthy
hard	heavy
head	happy
high	hello

You may also give other words and ask students to tell "h" words which are opposite of the words you name:

cold	sick
soft	light
foot	sad
low	good-bye

"H" Objects

Ask, "Can you tell me about any of the following things?" (Make a note of those things that no one can describe and provide pictures at a later date.)

hammer	hedge	harp	harmonica
hammock	holster	helmet	hamper
hatchet	holly	hut	hoe
hive	harness	hoof	hook

Tongue Twisters

- Ask the children to repeat in unison after you. Then ask if anyone would like to try to say a tongue twister as fast as possible alone.

    Hungry hounds howl and hunt.   *Happy Heather hugged Harriet.*
    Henry Horse had a huge harness.   *Handsome Harry Hedgehog hurried home.*
    Hubert Hare hops hurdles.   *Helen Hornet's head hurts.*

- Now ask the children to add one or more "h" words to the following to make tongue twisters.

    Humpty Dumpty hurried...   *Holly Hawk hunts...*
    Heather hears...   *Horrible Hank has...*
    Hand the handkerchief to...   *Harvey hollered...*

- Tell the children to answer "yes" or "no" to these questions and to explain why they answered as they did.

    Can a heel howl?   *Can a horse halt?*
    Can a hurricane hike?   *Could a husband hit a hornet?*
    Can hay be piled in a heap?   *Can a highway hunt?*
    Can you hear a hook?   *Is a hippopotamus heavy?*

"H" Art and Activities

Use Your Senses

Sense of Touch and Smell

1. Duplicate the letter H on page 87.
2. Cover with glue. Sprinkle with hay or hickory chips.
3. Have students close their eyes and then feel and smell the letter.

Sense of Taste

Let students taste different heart candies. Children tell what flavor they think they are. Also let them taste honeydew melon. Some might like to dip theirs into honey.

Sense of Hearing

Ask children to imitate a hiss, howl, and hoot. Then ask them what animals make these sounds.

Sense of Sight

Play "I Spy." When children are out of the room, place items beginning with the letter "h" in clear view. Items around the room might include hammer, hanger, hook, hat, hood, hoop, and handkerchief. When students return, begin a game by saying, "I spy an 'h' object in the room…" and give a clue to its identity (i.e., "…that you might wear on your head"). The student who guesses correctly may then say "I spy." An adult may need to whisper a suggestion for an object or clue.

Hedgehog

You may wish to show the children a picture of a true hedgehog. They have spiny hairs on their back and sides and are found in Europe, but not in America. They should not be confused with porcupines. Read aloud *The Tale of Mrs. Tiggy Winkle*, by Beatrix Potter (Warne, 1905).

Students can make "hedgehogs" of their own. Slice a potato in half lengthwise. (Each potato will make two hedgehogs.) Students can lay the potatoes on the cut side and poke toothpicks into the back and sides of them. Legs are made with larger sticks (broken match or ice cream sticks). Attach paper fasteners, thumb tacks or glue on paper for eyes. Use the hedgehogs for free play and/or to act out the story above.

Hat Day

The day before this activity, send a note home to parents explaining to them about hat day. Let them know that each child should wear a special hat. It could be his or her own or one belonging to someone in the family. Each student should be prepared to tell the class why his hat is special.

Make Hats

Give each student a paper plate and let him attach ribbon or yarn to the sides of the paper plate. The pieces of ribbon should be long enough to allow the student to tie the ends together under his chin with the plate on his head. Students can decorate the hats and have a hat show.

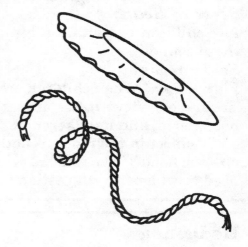

Here are some ideas for types of hats and items they should include:

Happy Hat—smiling faces
Healthy Hat—good foods
Hearty Hat—hearts
Horse Hat—horse ears on top

Hand Activities

Hand Impressions

Make hand impressions. Use your own clay recipe or the one on page 35. Flatten a ball into a circle about ½ inch thick and slightly larger than the child's hand. Lightly powder the child's hand and have him press it into the circle until it makes a clear impression. You may wish to poke a hole above the fingers so it can be hung up later. Place the finished work on a cake rack and let it dry for two days. It can be left plain or decorated using paints or markers.

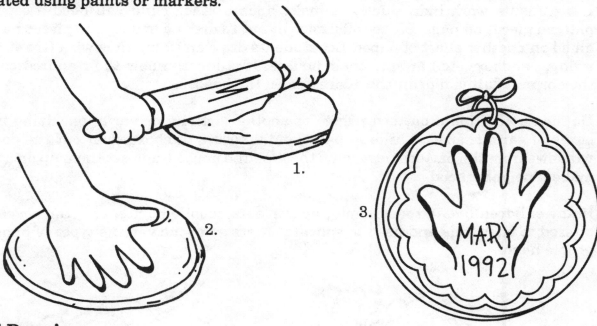

1.

2.

3.

Hand Drawings

Let students draw outlines of their hands. Working with partners makes it easier. After they have made outlines of their hands, let them add detail to turn the outline into a part of a different picture. Here are some examples:

Houses

Read aloud *A House is a House for Me,* by Mary Ann Hoberman (Viking Press, 1978), and *The Little House,* by Virginia Lee Burton (Houghton Mifflin, 1942).

Model Houses

Let students work individually to make houses. Each child will need a copy of the pattern pieces on page 95 to color and cut out to make a house. The pieces need to be glued on another sheet of paper. Let students draw anything they wish (trees, bushes, swing, sandbox, etc.) around their houses. If students know their addresses, either they or an adult can print the addresses on the houses.

Duplicate additional pattern pages for another activity or variation. Bring in small boxes of various sizes. Children paint and decorate the boxes, cut out the doors and windows from the pattern page, glue these on the houses, and set them up on a table to make a neighborhood.

If any children live in town homes, apartments, mobile homes, etc., the boxes can be altered to show this and used to educate others as to the various types of homes that people have.

H-House Pattern

Honeybees

Visit a demonstration beehive in your community if you have one, or invite a bee-keeper to the classroom. Ask him to bring some of the equipment that is used to raise honeybees. At the end of the activities, children should realize that people do not make honey. Bees gather nectar from flowers and store it in their bodies where it changes into honey.

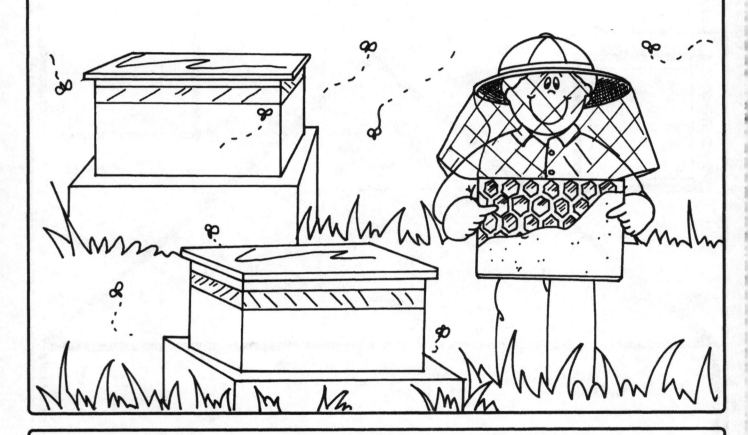

Movement
- Have hopping races (feet together, left foot, right foot).
- Jump over some very low hurdles.
- Demonstrate hopscotch.
- Play a simple handball game. An adult can pitch a large soft ball to a child. The child hits it with his hand, runs to one base and then home.
- Take a hike. Look for hills, including ant hills and heaps of dirt.

Music
Bring in horns, a horn player and/or pictures of horns (french horn, bugles, trumpet, hunting horn, coaching horn, etc.). Listen to recordings of horn music. Compare sounds. You may also have your class hum some familiar tunes.

"H" Games

Drop the Handkerchief

Players all sit in a circle except the one chosen to be "it." That person carries a handkerchief and quickly moves around the outside of the circle, dropping the handkerchief behind one player. As soon as the handkerchief is dropped, "it" runs and the seated player picks it up and chases "it" trying to tag him before he reaches the player's place and sits down. If the player catches "it," he must drop the handkerchief again. If not, the player is the new "it."

Hot Potato

Players stand close together in a circle and pass a potato or some other object that is easily passed. "It" stands outside and faces away from the circle. When he calls, "Stop," the one holding the potato may not pass it and becomes the new "it." Variation—"It" plays music while children pass object. When he stops music, the one with the object becomes "It." With older children, the one caught can leave the game until there are only two players left and finally one winner.

Heads Up, Heads Down

Select 4 to 6 children to go to the front of the room and one of them to be the leader. The leader says, "Heads down." All seated players fold their arms around their heads and hide their eyes . Each standing child moves around the room and gently taps the head of one of the children. Immediately, the child with head down puts up one finger so he will not be tapped a second time. When all tappers are finished and up front, the leader says, "Heads up," and the children who were tapped stand and one at a time guess who tapped them. If correct, they exchange places for the next game.

"H" Food

"Hoe" Cake

Make cornbread from a package mix and serve it to the children from a hoe. Explain that the early settlers baked this on a hoe and that is why it is so named. You can spread honey or honey butter on the "hoe" cake.

Heart, Hand Cookies

Use prepared, rolled cookie dough or your favorite recipe for rolled cookies. Use a heart shaped cookie cutter or make a paper pattern to cut around. If possible, let children cut out their own cookies. If no stove is available, bake a few at a time in a toaster oven. Have each child lay his hand on the rolled dough (or make a paper pattern of each), cut out the shape, and cook. Have students keep track of the location of their cookies on the tray since they change shape during cooking. Frost and decorate the hands and hearts.

Honey Butter

To make honey butter, use beaters and whip ¼ pound of butter with ¼ cup of honey. Children might like to make their own butter.

Butter

The fast way to make butter is to use beaters or a blender and whip ¼ pound of whipping cream until butter forms. If you would like to get the children involved, put the whipping cream in a clear plastic container with a very tight lid. Have the children sit in a circle and pass the container, each taking a turn shaking it until a ball of butter is sitting in liquid. (This may take 4 or 5 minutes.) Pour off the liquid, add a little salt or make into honey butter and spread.

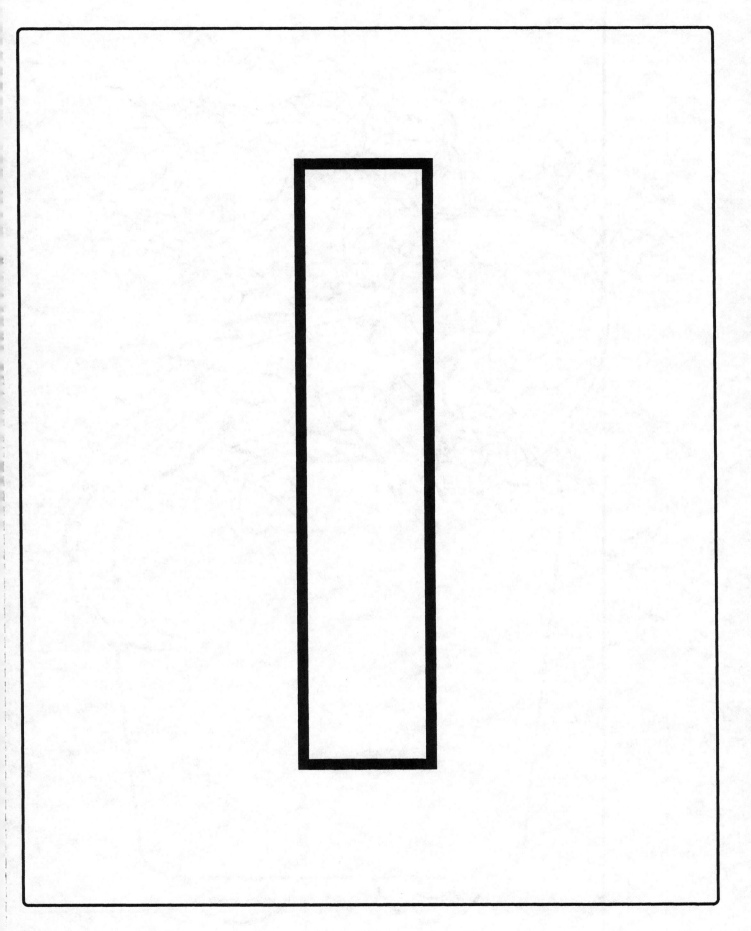

100

"I" Vocabulary and Oral Expression

Introducing "I"

Introduce "i" words through conversation, illustrations, and questions. (Does anyone have an infant in his home? Can you imitate an animal? Who can tell their initials?)

Names	Animals	Opposites
Ian	inchworm	indoors—outdoors
Ira	iguana	inhale—exhale
Ivan	ibis	ill—well
Irvin	insect	in—out
Irma		is—isn't (is not)
Iris		inside—outside
Irene		idle—busy
		interesting—uninteresting

outside   inside

Tongue Twisters

- Ask children to repeat in unison after you. Then ask if anyone would like to try to say a tongue twister as fast as possible alone.

  The infant is imitating Iris.
  Is an igloo icy?
  Is it impolite to interrupt?

  Ian is injured.
  Ivory is interesting,
  The insect bite made Irma itch.

- Tell the children to answer "yes" or "no" to these questions and to explain why they answered as they did.

  Can an inch iron?
  Could you imitate an insect?
  Could an igloo be improved?
  Could ice skates get icy?

  Would you iron an idea?
  Could you write initials in ink?
  Can ice cream be ill?
  Could you be in an inn?

"I" Objects

Ask, "Can you tell me about any of the following things?"
(Make a note of those things that no one can describe and
provide pictures at a later date.)

ice skates	igloo	inch
insect	ink	iron
ivy	ice	ivory
island	icicle	inn

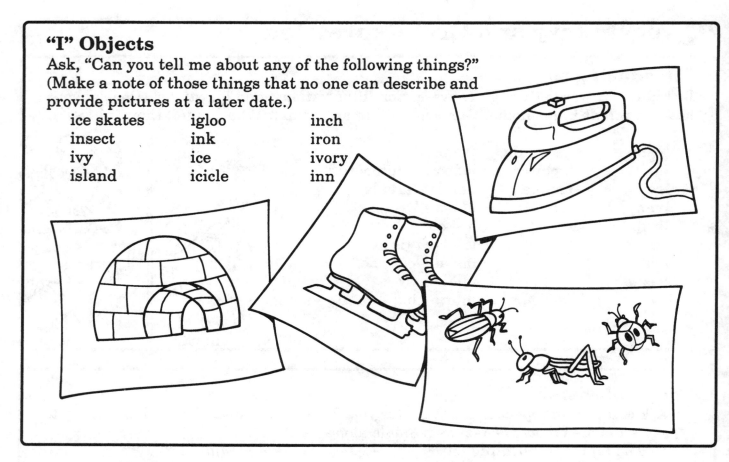

"I" Art and Activities

Use Your Senses

Sense of Touch and Smell
1. Duplicate the letter "I" on page 99.
2. Cover it with glue. Sprinkle with incense.
3. Have students close their eyes and then feel and smell the page.

Sense of Taste
Freeze flavored ice cubes (lemon, grape, cherry, etc.). Insert an ice cream stick before completely frozen or wrap in napkin for tasting ease. Ask children to identify the flavors of the ice.

Sense of Hearing
Listen to a tape or recording featuring different musical instruments. See how many the children can identify the first time. Give them the names of those that no one knows. Then play again and see how many more they now can identify by sound.

Sense of Sight
Play "I Spy." When children are out of the room, place items beginning with the letter "I" in clear view (ivy, ink, inch, iron, etc.). When students return, begin a game by saying, "I spy an 'i' object in the room..." and giving a clue to its identity (i.e., "that you might use to measure something"). The student who guesses correctly may then say "I spy." An adult may need to whisper a suggestion for an object or a clue.

Insects

Have pictures to identify and pass around. If live insects can be located, pass them around in clear containers while you discuss and ask questions. (Good examples are ants, crickets, grasshoppers and flies.)

	True Insects
Can anyone count how many legs each insect has?	have 6
Can you see three body parts?	have 3
What are antennae? Do you see any?	have 2

If you have live insects, ask the children to observe how they move and if anyone can imitate that movement.

Let students make insects from salt clay (recipe on page 35). Have each child form three body parts and add six toothpick legs and two antennae.

Imagination

Review and discuss the meaning of the word *imagination*. Tell the children to close their eyes and imagine a new insect that has never been seen before. Tell them they may draw this imaginary insect or they may color, cut out and paste on a sheet of paper the body parts, legs, and antennae provided on this page. If they choose to draw, they should be reminded that their insects should have three body parts, six legs, and two antennae.

Duplicate the legs, antennae, and body parts below for each student.

Insect Fingerprints

Let children make their fingerprints by pressing each finger on an ink pad. Make the fingerprints into insects by adding six legs and antennae.

Igloo

Show children pictures of igloos. Discuss who lives in them. Have each child build an igloo using marshmallows and toothpicks. Make a thick mixture of powdered sugar and water. Have them put the mixture over the igloos to look like snow. The students may then eat their igloos.

Initials

Make your favorite modeling dough recipe or use the one on page 35. Children can roll the dough into long, thin rolls, break it into sections and form the letters that are their initials. Copies of their initials may help the children form their letters correctly.

Invisible Art

Put lemon juice in small bowls. Give the children clean brushes and have them draw pictures and practice forming the letter "I." Tell them that the juice will look invisible (discuss meaning), but that you will make it appear. Iron with a warm (not hot) iron or hold over a lightbulb. As the juice turns brown, the picture will appear!

An Inch

How big is an inch? Cut out a piece of paper that is one square inch for each child or duplicate the one at right. Send children on a hunt (inside or outside) looking for things that are an inch long. Then look for objects that are bigger than an inch and then objects that are smaller than an inch.

Inches

Duplicate and ask children to cut out the six-inch ruler below. Precut cardboard the same length as the rulers. Direct each child to glue his ruler to a strip of cardboard. Demonstrate how to use the ruler to measure and do some of the activities on the following page.

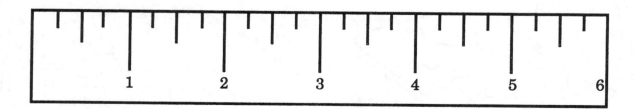

Inches

Have students use the rulers from the previous page to measure the following things:

> their little fingers
> their longest fingers
> their crayons, pencils, scissors

Have them look around the room and find something that is

> longer than six inches
> shorter than six inches

Allow children time to look at foot rulers and yard sticks. Ask them to count aloud with you the number of inches in each. Ask measurement questions such as the following:

> Which is longer, an inch or a foot?
> Which is shorter, a yard or a foot?
> From where you are sitting, what can you see that is longer than six inches?
> What can you see that is shorter than six inches?
> Do you think that you are taller than this yardstick (hold perpendicular to the floor) or shorter? Check and see.

Inchworm home

Glue dirt to brown butcher paper. Lay out on a table or tack to a bulletin board. Ask each child to draw, color, and cut out an "inchworm." Students can glue them in their dirt "homes."

Ice

Ice Shapes

To do this activity, you will need access to a freezer. Gather a number of small, unbreakable containers of various shapes. Some things to use are balloons, paper cups, and small milk containers. Direct the children to fill them with water and place them in the freezer. Allow them to check the freezing process periodically to observe which ones freeze first and which parts remain liquid the longest. When all shapes are frozen solid, remove the ice from the container (or cut away the container if using a balloon, paper cup, or small milk container). Place the shapes in a deep tray and let the children discuss and touch them. Let students periodically inspect the shapes throughout the melting process. Discuss why certain shapes and parts melt first.

Alternate idea—Freeze some shapes. Remove from containers out of sight of children. Ask them to match the ice shapes to the correct containers.

Ice Melts

You will need: ice cubes, identical in size

1 paper cup per child with the child's name on the side

Put an ice cube in each cup and ask the children to place the cup where they think the ice will melt quickly. Observe which one melts first and discuss why. Do the activity again and have students place their ice where they think it will take the longest to melt. This activity might also be done outside during a playground period.

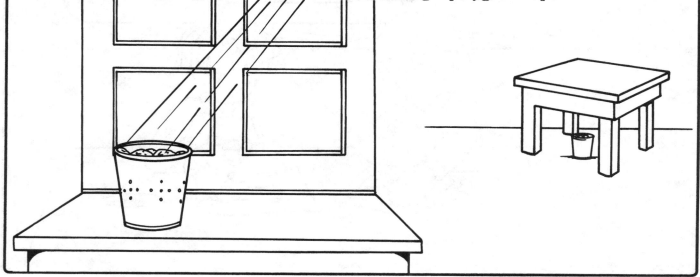

Ice Art

You will need: melting ice cubes
glossy paper
dry tempera paint
(one or more colors)

Demonstrate how to sprinkle the dry paint over the paper. Have each child take a melting ice cube and let the drops fall on the paint. If children find it difficult to hold the cold ice, wrap one end in a napkin or cloth. It may be necessary to rub the cube or dip in warm water to keep it melting. The water on the dry paint will create a design on the paper. Allow to dry. Hold painting over a newspaper and shake gently to remove any dry paint remaining.

"I" Food

Ice slush

You will need: manual or automatic ice crushers
fruit juices and/or syrups
paper cups
spoons
ice cubes

If you have the facilities, give each child the opportunity to crush at least one ice cube. Put the crushed ice in the cups and pack firmly. Let each child select his favorite juice or syrup to pour over the slush.

Making Ice Cream

There is water in milk and cream. When this water freezes, it becomes solid ice crystals. When making ice cream you will want to make these ice crystals as small as possible. To prevent large ice crystals from forming, freeze the ice cream as quickly as possible and beat it while it is freezing. This way the frozen water will spread out evenly and the ice cream will be smooth. An ice cream freezer that whips the ice cream as it freezes makes the best ice cream. If one is not available to you, you can make some in the freezer section of a refrigerator. It will taste good but it will not be as creamy. If using an electric freezer, follow the manufacturer's directions.

Refrigerator Tray Peppermint Ice Cream

You will need:
2 envelopes of unflavored gelatin
1 cup cold milk
3 cups hot milk
2 ½ cups of crushed peppermint stick candy
4 cups whipping cream (stiffly whipped)
½ teaspoon salt

Soften the gelatin by placing it in a bowl with the cold milk. Then add the hot milk (scalded) and stir until all the gelatin is dissolved. Add ½ teaspoon salt and all but ½ cup of the crushed candy to the hot milk mixture. Stir to dissolve. Freeze in a refrigerator tray. Make sure the dial on the freezer compartment is turned to the coldest temperature possible. Once frozen, break up and beat the mixture smooth with an electric mixer. Fold in the whipped cream and the remaining candy. You may wish to add a little red food coloring. Freeze again in the refrigerator tray. This will make up to sixteen servings.

Ice Cream Cone Cupcakes

Prepare a packaged cake mix according to directions. Place flat-bottomed ice cream cones in the holes of muffin tins and fill up halfway with batter. Bake 15 to 18 minutes at 400°. Allow children to ice the cupcakes when they have cooled. Add sprinkles, candies, nuts, or fruits. Children could make the icing.

Initial Cookies

Use prepared cookie dough (available in the refrigerator case at the grocery store). Roll out according to package directions. Let children use letter cookie cutters or letter pattern cut-outs from this book to form their initials in the dough. If no large oven is available, bake a few at a time in a toaster oven. Let children make icing to ice their initial cookies.

Instant Pudding

Discuss the meaning of the word "instant." Following the package directions, let children help prepare several flavors of instant puddings. They will probably disappear instantly.

Ice Cream Sandwiches

Prepare large flat cookies (two per child), several flavors of ice cream in bowls, and dull knives for spreading. Let each child prepare his own ice cream sandwich by spreading ice cream on one cookie and putting the second on top.

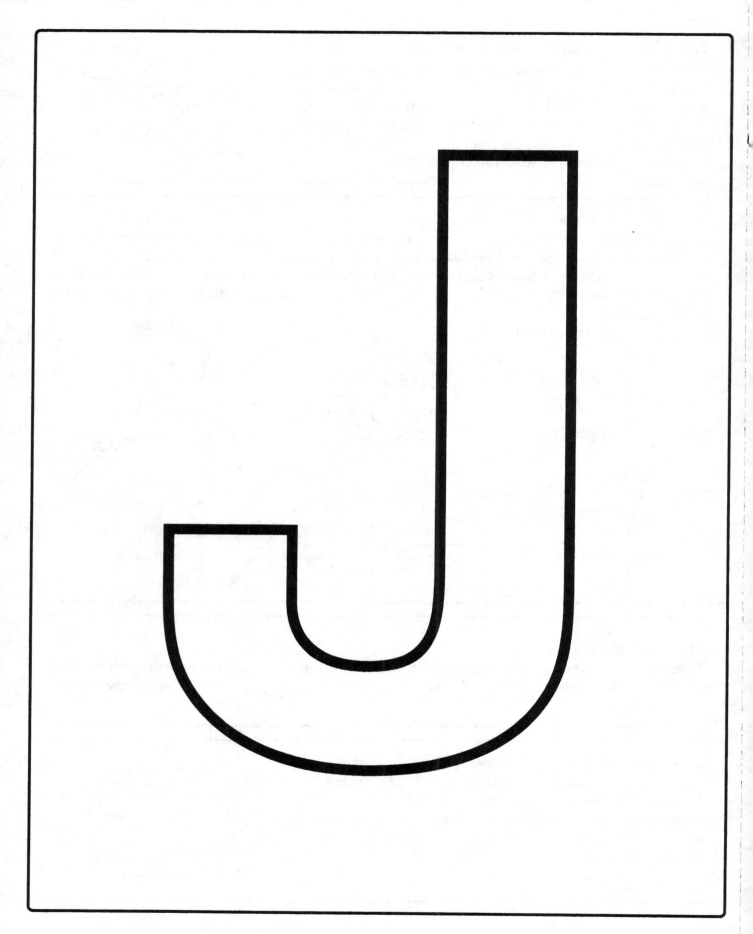

112

113

"J" Vocabulary and Oral Expression

Introducing "J"

Introduce "j" words through conversation, illustrations, and questions. (What does a jockey do? How would you make a jack-o'-lantern? Do you know how to play the game called "jacks"?)

Names

Jodie	James	Jason	Joy	Jay
Jack	Joel	John	Joyce	Jane
Julia	Jerry	Jonathan	Joshua	June
Justin	Jessie	Janet	Janice	Joel
Jean	Jenny	Jessica	Jill	Joan

What things do students know that could do the following:

joke	jump
jiggle	jog
juggle	

"J" Objects

Ask, "Can you tell me about any of the following things?" (Make a note of those things that no one can describe and provide pictures at a later date.)

jelly	jaw	jet
jaguar	jeep	jail
jewelry	jungle	jeans
jack-in-the-box	juggler	

114

Tongue Twisters

- Ask the children to repeat in unison after you. Then ask if anyone would like to try to say a tongue twister as fast as possible alone.

  Jim tells jolly jokes.   *Joyce Johnson joined the joggers.*

  Jerry's jeep jiggles.   *Jack's jaw was covered with jelly.*

  Julie's job is juggling.   *Jay Jaguar jogged through the jungle.*

- Now ask students to add one or more "j" words to the following to make tongue twisters;

  Jason juggles.........   *The jolly jeweler...*

  Jonathan Jones...   *The jelly in the jar...*

  Jello...   *Jockey John put the junk in the...*

- Tell the children to answer "yes" or "no" to these questions and to explain why they answered as they did.

  Can a jail jump?   *Could a jockey jog?*

  Could a jet juggle?   *Could a jackknife jab?*

  Does junk jiggle?   *Could a jeweler tell a joke?*

  Can you put jelly in a jar?   *Could you carry juice in a jeep?*

"J" Art and Activities

Use Your Senses

Sense of Touch and Smell
1. Duplicate the letter "J" on page 112.
2. Cover it with glue. Sprinkle with powdered gelatin.
3. Have students close their eyes and then feel and smell the page.

Sense of Hearing
Bring in different sizes of bells to jingle. Have children close their eyes. See if they can hear the difference in sound when small bells are jingled and when large ones are jingled. Talk about and experiment with other things that jingle, such as keys.

Sense of Taste
Have children close their eyes and taste a jellybean. (Use common flavors.) See if they can determine what flavor they are tasting.

Sense of Sight
When children are out of the room, place items beginning with the letter "j" in clear view (jack-in-the-box, jar of jelly or jam, a jug, jacks, etc.). When students return, begin a game by saying, "I spy a 'j' object in the room…" and giving a clue to its identity (i.e., "…that you might put on a sandwich"). The student who guesses correctly may then say "I spy." An adult may need to whisper a suggestion for an object or clue.

Make Jewelry
Send a note home asking for donations of old beads, jewelry, and shoelaces. Take apart the old jewelry and save the pieces to be restrung. Let children use dental floss (for small holes) and shoelaces to string beads and make their own bracelets and necklaces. If pins, earrings, etc., are donated, save them for playing jewelry store or dress-up.

Joke Day
Keeping in mind the level of students' sense of humor, read selected jokes from your favorite joke book, *What Do You Hear When Cows Sing? And Other Silly Riddles* by Marco and Giulio Maestro (HarperCollins, 1997), or *Kids' Silliest Jokes* by Jacqueline Horsfall (Sterling, 2003). Tell children that tomorrow will be "Joke Day" and each one of them may tell a joke to the class. A note home to the parents would be helpful as they could give suggestions and an opportunity to practice.

Jack-in-the-box

Have each child make a jack-in-the-box using the pattern on page 119. Have them decorate, color, and cut out the pattern pieces. Then, fold along the dotted lines and tape together the large piece to make the box. Accordion fold the short rectangular strip. Tape one end to the bottom of the character back and the other end to the inside of the box.

Juggling

Stuff one sock into another. Roll it up to make a ball. Let students try juggling two sock balls.

Jumping

Have the students jump with their feet together, forward, backward, sideways, and with a turn. You may also have jumping races.

Jumping Jacks

Teach children how to do jumping jacks. They should jump so that their legs go apart and hands go over the head at the same time. Some very young children may have difficulty doing both at the same time.

Jump Rope

Demonstrate how to jump rope. Most very young children do not have the coordination to do this, but they can jump over the rope if you stretch it across the floor. Then try raising it a little and tying it to the legs of two chairs. Some will be able to jump over this.

Giant Jam Sandwich

Read aloud *The Giant Jam Sandwich,* by John Vernon Lord (Houghton Mifflin, 1973). Have a slice of bread for each child, dull knives for spreading, and jars of jelly and jam. Ask each child to spread jelly or jam on his bread. Then make a giant sandwich by piling the slices on top of each other. Press down on the slices. Lay the finished sandwich on its side, and cut off a section for each child.

Join the Band

One child is selected to be the "band leader" and stands in the middle of the room. All the other children stand on one side of the room with their backs against the wall. If played outside, establish start and finish lines. The band leader calls out, "Here I stand! Here I stand! Who will come and join my band? I clap my hands! I clap my hands!"

The leader then claps his hands, and the other children must run across to the opposite wall. As they are running, the leader tries to catch them before they touch the other wall. Any child he tags joins his band and stands with him in the middle of the room. All the new band members try to tag children. The game continues until all the children are tagged. The last child caught is the winner and becomes the new leader of the band.

118

Jack-in-the-box Pattern

119

Juice Can Holder

Ask children to bring in an empty 12-oz. juice can. Decorate the rectangle below, cut it out, and glue it around the can. Use at school or as a gift.

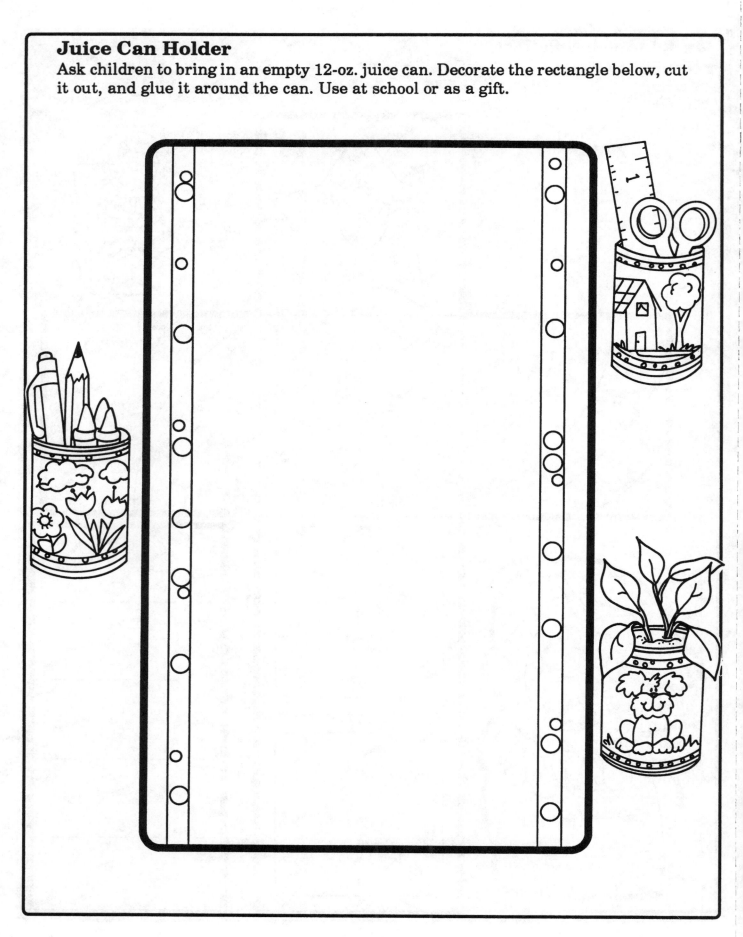

"J" Foods

Juices

Bring in various fruits, a blender, crushed ice, and cups for tasting. Let children touch, smell and taste bite sized pieces of each whole fruit. Then blend ½ cup of cut up fruit with ¼ cup crushed ice. Give each child a cup of each juice to sip. Compare the taste of the juice with the bite of the whole fruit.

Jiggling "J"s

Prepare gelatin according to package directions. Pour into very shallow pans to set. When firm, cut into the letter "j" using a knife or letter cookie cutter. Remove each letter with a spatula and serve one to each child.

No-Cook Jam

You will need a quart of fruit (blackberries, raspberries, blueberries, sour cherries, peaches, or strawberries), sugar, lemon juice and fruit pectin (available in grocery stores in powdered or liquid form). If you wish to let children take home a sample, prepare small jars with tight fitting lids by running them through an automatic dishwasher with a very hot rinse. Follow the directions included in the pectin container. The directions vary according to the type of fruit pectin you buy. This is an excellent activity since it involves no cooking, but the children will have opportunities to measure, stir, set a timer, and ladle the mixture into containers. Tell them to store their samples in their refrigerators at home.

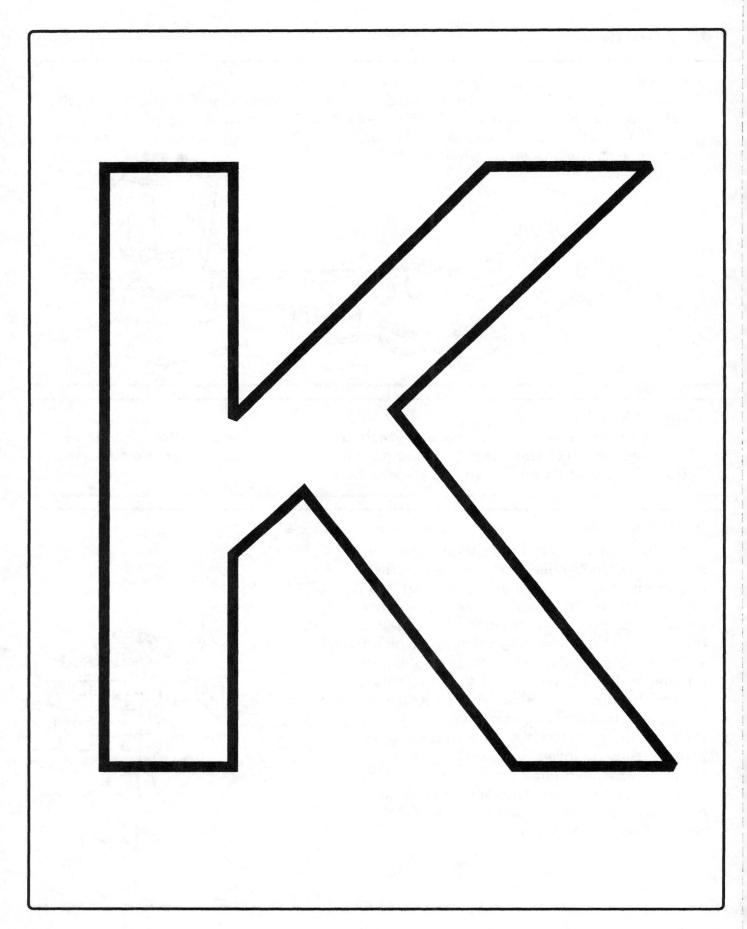

122

"K" Vocabulary and Oral Expression

Introducing "K"

Introduce "k" words through conversation, illustrations, and questions. (Do you know some games where players kick a ball? What would you expect to see at a kennel? Where do they have workers that are sometimes called "keepers"?)

Names

Kay	Karen
Kristen	Kelly
Kevin	Karl
Karla	Keith
Kenny	Kitty
Katy	Kathy

Kn words that sound like "N"

knife	knock
knee	knob
knapsack	kneel
knight	knit
know	knew
knot	knuckles

Animals

kangaroo	kitten
koala	katydid

Homonyms ("N" sound)

knight-night
know-no
knew-new

"K" Objects

Ask, "Can you tell me about any of the following things?" (Make a note of those things that no one can describe and provide pictures at a later date.)

kayak	kitchen
key	keyhole
kite	kaleidoscope
keg	king

("N" sound)

knot	knitting
knuckles	knob

Tongue Twisters

- Ask children to repeat in unison after you. Then ask if anyone would like to try to say a tongue twister as fast as possible alone.

    Katie Kangaroo keeps kicking.   *Kevin and Kris kissed the kittens.*
    Karl put the key in the keyhole.   *Karla and Kenny are in kindergarten.*
    The keeper of the kennels has the keys. *Ned knots his knapsack.* ("N" sound)

- Now ask the children if they can add one or more "k" words to the following to make tongue twisters.

    Kenneth keeps Kelly's...
    Karl kissed baby...
    Kitty kicked the...
    Kathy put the kit in the kitchen for...

- Tell the children to answer "yes" or "no" to these questions and to explain why they answered as they did.

    Do you think you might see a kettle in a kitchen?
    Can a kit and a kid both be baby animals?
    Could a kangaroo use a kaleidoscope?
    Is a keg a kind of kitten?
    Can you kick a kite?

"K" Activities

Use Your Senses

Sense of Touch
1. Duplicate the letter "K" on page 122.
2. Cover with glue. Sprinkle with a crispy cereal.
3. Have students close their eyes and feel the page.

Sense of Taste
Have children close their eyes and then give each one a candy kiss (chocolate, peanut butter, etc.). See if they can determine the flavor by tasting only.

Sense of Hearing
- Ask one child to go where no one can see him and to knock a specific number of times. The other children should listen carefully, and tell the number of knocks.
- After the children make the kazoos (page 129), ask each one to hum a familiar tune into their kazoo. The other children should listen to see if they can recognize the melody.

Sense of Sight
- Bring in a kaleidoscope. Pass it to each child and ask him to describe the design he sees.
- Play, "I Spy." When children are out of the room, place items beginning with the letter "k" in clear view. You might include a kite, keys, or pictures of kangaroos or kittens. When students are in the room, begin a game by saying, "I spy a 'k' object in the room..." and give a clue to its identity (i.e., "...that you might use to unlock something"). The student who guesses correctly may then say "I spy." An adult may need to whisper a suggestion for an object or clue.

"K" Movement

Kicking
Have children stand in two lines that face each other and practice kicking a ball back and forth so it moves up and down the lines.
Have students practice kicking a ball into a soccer goal. A goal can be made using two sticks and a net or piece of cloth.

Play "Keep Away"
Two players throw a ball back and forth to each other. A third player stands between them and tries to intercept it. If he is successful, he exchanges places with the one who threw the ball.

Kite Day
Send home a note asking parents to let children bring in any kites they have at home. Have some adults to help (or older children, if available) and fly as many kites as your space and adult help will allow. Weather conditions may determine the scheduling of this activity.

"K" Games

Hide the King's Keys

Color and cut out the keys on page 128. (You may wish to duplicate the crown since it can also be used in the next activity, King Lion.) Punch a hole in each key, and thread on a chain, ribbon or yarn. One person will hide the keys and may wear the crown. All other players hide their eyes. When the keys are "hidden" (actually they need to be in plain sight, but in an odd place), the king says, "Find the king's keys." Everyone starts to hunt without talking. When someone sees the keys, he takes his seat and waits until everyone has seen them. The king then selects one player to go get the keys and puts the crown on his head as the new king.

King Lion

The children should sit in a circle with their chairs facing outward. One child has no chair and is given the crown from page 128 which has a picture of a lion on it. This child is the King Lion. All the other players have a picture of an animal taped to them or they could also wear crowns with their animal glued on them. The King Lion walks around the circle, calling out the names of some of the animals he sees. The child who is wearing that picture gets up and marches behind the king. At any time, the king may yell, "I'm hungry," and start to run. The children behind him start to run also and when the king sits down in an empty chair, the others who are up quickly try to find a seat too. One will be left with no seat. That child is the new King Lion.

K-Crown and Key Patterns

Use these patterns to play "Hide the King's Keys" and "King Lion."

Crown

Color and cut out the crown pattern. Cut a long strip of paper and glue the crown to the center. Adjust the strip to fit a child's head and staple into a circle.

Keys

Color and cut out the keys. You may wish to mount on heavy paper and laminate. Punch a hole in the top of each key and string on a chain, yarn or ribbon.

Lion

King

"K" Activities

Make a Kazoo

You will need: empty tubes from paper products
waxed paper
rubber band (one for each kazoo)

Punch a pencil size hole in one end of the tube.
Cover the other end with a piece of waxed paper.
Use a rubber band to hold the waxed paper in
place. Students can hum tunes into the uncovered
ends of their kazoos.

Kangaroo Race

Divide children into teams. Establish start
and finish lines. Give a small, soft ball to the
first player on each team. When given the
signal to start, that player puts the ball between his knees and, moving both feet together, hops to the finish line. If the ball
falls, he picks it up, puts it back between his
knees, and continues on. When he reaches
the finish line, he puts the ball in his hand
and runs back and gives it to the second
player on his team. The race continues until
everyone has a turn, and the winning team
is the one that finishes first.

Poor Kitty

One child is chosen to be the kitty. The rest of the players sit in a circle. Kitty crawls
around the inside of the circle on hands and knees and stops at each seated player,
saying, "Meow" (pretending to be sad, lonely, hungry, or whatever the student wishes).
After the "Meow," the person approached
must pet the kitty's head and say,
"Poor kitty." The person petting
the kitty must keep a straight face
while saying this. If the person
laughs or smiles, that person is
the new kitty.

"K" Foods

Snack Kabobs

You will need: wooden skewers or
           sandwich picks (1 per child)
           cubes of snack items such as
                cooked cold meat
                cherry tomatoes
                olives
                cheese
                pickles
                peppers

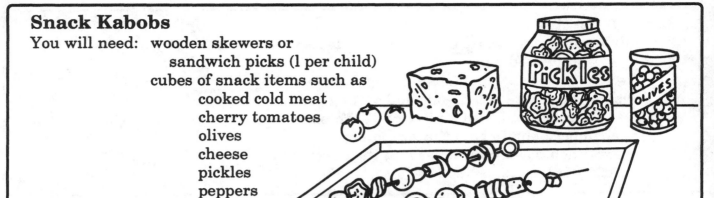

You might find out from the children what soft foods they like other than those listed above. Allow each child to fix his own kabob. Encourage students to try at least one new food. Some may need help putting their items on the skewers. They should remove the items and put on a plate before attempting to eat.

A variation of this activity would be to make fruit kabobs.

Krispy "K's"

You will need: ¼ cup butter (and some extra to put on hands)
           1 large package regular marshmallows
           5 cups of a krispy cereal

Melt the butter and add the marshmallows. Stir until melted. Remove from heat and stir in cereal. Put butter on hands and mold mixture into several large "K" shapes. Place on wax paper to cool. If allowed to cool slightly, some children might enjoy trying to mold their own letters. Cut up the K's and let your class have them for a krispy snack.

"L" Vocabulary and Oral Expression

Introducing "L"

Introduce "l" words through conversation, illustrations, and questions. (Can you describe the color lavender? Can you tell me something that is a liquid? Why would you need luggage?)

Names		Opposites		Foods	Animals
Laura	Larry	low—high	love-hate	lettuce	lamb
Lee	Leo	loud—soft	lost-found	lemon	leopard
Leah	Lester	loose—tight	long-short	lime	lizard
Leslie	Louise	light—heavy	light-dark	liver	llama
Libby	Lionel	large—small	late-early	lima beans	locust
Lilly	Lloyd	laugh—cry	leave-stay		lion
Linda	Luke	left—right			loon
Lisa	Luther				
Lois	Loretta				
Louise	Lucy				
Lynn	Lonnie				

LILY LAKE

"L" Adjectives

Ask children to name things that fit the following descriptions:

large	limp
long	loose
light	

What things do they know that they can label? that they can lock? that they can loan? that they can lift?

"L" Objects

Ask, "Can you tell me about any of the following things?" (Make a note of those things that no one can describe and provide pictures at a later date.)

lace	ladybug	lantern
luggage	lake	leaf
lodge	leather	litter
lumber	lawn	leash
liter	locker	log
letter	list	

Tongue Twisters

- Ask children to repeat in unison after you. Then ask if anyone would like to try to say a tongue twister as fast as possible alone.

  Lazy Laura left the laundry.   *Lee eats lemon lady-fingers.*
  Lois Lamb got loose.   *Low lanterns lit the lodge.*
  Lucky Larry laughed loudly.   *Later Lucy lit the lamp.*

- Now ask the children to add one or more "l" words to the following to make tongue twisters.

  Leslie and Lewis...
  Luke loaned his lock to...
  Lester left...
  Libby lost her...
  Lisa lifted...
  Lloyd likes...

- Tell the children to answer "yes" or "no" to these questions and to explain why they answered as they did.

  Would you put a leash on a lizard?   *Could a lawyer be lonely?*
  Could you buy a liter of lightning?   *Does a ladder have a lid?*
  Can a lemon look at a lime?   *Does a letter have legs?*
  Do leaves sometimes lie on the lawn?   *Do you think you could lift a light log?*

"L" Art and Activities

Use Your Senses

Sense of Touch and Smell
1. Duplicate the letter "L" on page 131.
2. Cover it with glue. Sprinkle the letter with lemon or lime flavored powdered gelatin or drink mix.
3. Have students close their eyes, then feel and smell the page.

Sense of Taste
Ask children to close their eyes. Pass each one a lemon, licorice, or lime flavored lollipop or hard candy. Ask the children to taste them before opening their eyes to see if they can determine the flavor by taste alone.

Sense of Hearing
Compare low, high, loud, and soft notes. Have children close their eyes. Use a piano or sing. Tell them to raise their hands above their heads if they think the notes are high and to lower them to the floor if they sound low. Then have them listen to loud and soft notes. They can cover their ears with their hands if the notes are loud and cup their hands behind their ears if they are soft.

Sense of Sight
When children are out of the room, place items beginning with the letter "l" in clear view (lamp, light bulb, list and letters, etc.). When students return, begin a game by saying, "I spy an 'l' object in the room…" and give a clue to its identity (i.e., "…that you might write to a friend"). The student who guesses correctly may then say "I spy." An adult may need to whisper a suggestion for an object or clue.

Licorice Lady
Have a supply of licorice sticks, gumdrops, and toothpicks. Have children put together a licorice lady (flat on a paper plate since it will not stand). After walking around the room to see each other's creations, they can enjoy the licorice as tasting treats.

Learn to Lace

Duplicate the lacing shoe patterns below for students. You may wish to have the children color or decorate their copies. Cut and glue the patterns onto cardboard thin enough to punch. Allow to dry. Laminate if possible. Punch out the six holes on each shoe with a large paper punch. To lace, give the children old shoelaces or strips of yarn with the ends wrapped tightly with tape. Let them practice going in and out of the holes. Then give them a picture of criss-cross lacing or have shoes on display that are laced correctly for them to copy. Some might also learn to tie.

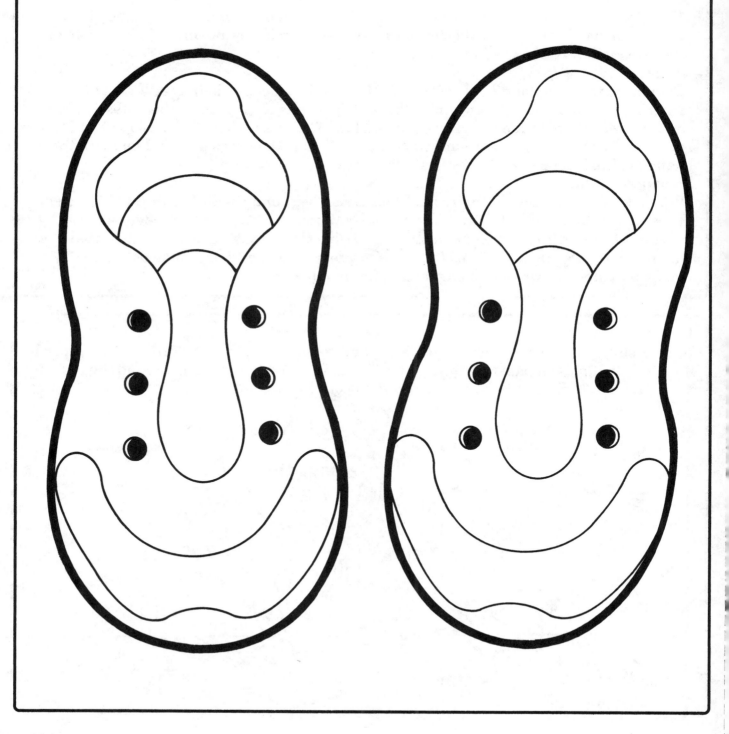

Ladybugs

Make rock ladybugs.
You will need: medium-sized smooth stones
(fairly flat on one side)
enamel paints
brushes
thinned shellac (optional)

Wash and completely dry the stones. Have some pictures and/or rocks completed to give children ideas that will help them make their ladybug rocks. They might like to practice on sheets of paper ahead of time. Have students paint the rocks to resemble ladybugs. After the paint is dry, you may apply a coat of thin shellac.

Visit the Library

Plan a visit to your school or public library. Ask the librarian to prepare a short program with "L" books and/or introducing "L" literary characters.

Lollipop Ladies

You will need: one lollipop for each child
                a copy of the pattern below for each child
                scrap materials for decorating
                    (felt, yarn, buttons, construction paper, etc.)

Tell the children to decorate the dress pattern below. Cut out on the dark, solid lines. Poke the end of the lollipop stick through the circle in the middle and pull the stick until it stops at the candy head. Glue the edges of the dress together. Use scraps to make the face, hands and hair.

fold →

138

Leaf Walk

Collect leaves from different trees in an area near your classroom. Place each on a separate piece of paper and laminate or cover with clear contact paper. Punch a hole in the top of each leaf card and string yarn through the hole, making it large enough to slip over a child's head. Have each child wear a leaf as you go for a walk. Stop at each tree and talk about the size and shape of the leaves. See if the children can match their leaves to the correct trees.

Leaf Rubbings

Pick up some extra leaves on your walk. Have each child place a leaf under a sheet of paper and, using the side of a crayon, rub over the leaf until the image of the leaf appears on the paper. They can do several on one sheet of paper with different colors making an interesting combination of colors and shapes.

Leaf Prints

Leaf prints can be made with a few children at a time or with the help of several adults.

You will need: leaves
               water based paint or ink
               a brayer (roller)
               cover-ups for each child
               newspapers
               paper to be printed

Place a leaf on newspaper. Pour a small amount of paint into a shallow paint container. Roll the brayer in the paint and apply to the leaf. Put the leaf paint-side down on paper. Put a sheet of newspaper on top of the leaf and press down, being careful not to move the leaf. Pick the leaf straight up to reveal the print.

Loop Art

Cut two or more strips of paper for each child. The strips should be two inches wide and of varying lengths (eight, ten, or twelve inches long). Tell the children to form the strips into loops. They may then glue the loops together to make animals, people or designs. Scrap paper can be available to make ears, tails, etc.

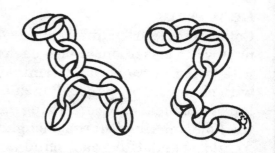

Light-Up Faces

Tell the children to draw and color a face on the bottom of a flat-bottomed lunch bag. Darken the room as much as possible and let each child "light up" his face and show it to the class by shining a flashlight into the bag and holding it up.

Play "L" Lotto

Make copies of pages 141 and 142 for each child. Tell the children to color each "l" object on page 142, cut out the completed pictures, and glue them at random to the spaces on their lotto board. This will make most boards different. Give students buttons, disks or scraps of paper as cover-ups. Ask a question whose answer is one of the "l" pictures. (*Which picture shows an animal called "The king of the beasts?"*) Children cover up the "l" picture described. The first one to get three in a row covered should call out, "Lotto." Play lotto several times and give a prize to each child for winning or being a good player.

140

Lotto Board Pattern

"L" LOTTO

Lotto Squares

light bulb

lion

lizard

leaf

lemon

ladybug

lettuce

leopard

lollipop

142

"L" Games

Leapfrog

Players form a line. If there is a great difference in height in the group, put the shorter players at the beginning of the line. The first player squats down, curling his head down toward the floor. The next player in line puts his hands on the back of the first, spreads his legs and leaps over. He then squats in front of the first player leaving some room between. (You might suggest six steps.) The third player leaps over both and squats. When all players are down, the last player can jump up and leap over them all, and then the next and so on. You can decide ahead of time how far or how long the leapfrog will go.

Follow the Leader

Indoors or out, the children line up behind the leader and imitate what he does. Everyone should have a turn being leader.

Guess the Leader

One child is chosen to be "it" and leaves the room. The remaining players sit on the floor in a circle. One of the seated children is selected as leader and starts and changes motions every few seconds which everyone else in the circle imitates (patting head, floor, rubbing hands, cheeks, etc.). The person playing "it" returns to the circle and tries to guess who is the leader. He has three guesses. If correct, that person becomes the new "it." If not, a new "it" is selected. Tell players not to look directly at the leader all the time.

"L" Food

Lemonade

To make lemonade, you will need: 5 or 6 lemons
sugar
water
ice
cups
squeezer

Children will enjoy taking turns squeezing the lemons. Add sugar to the lemon juice. (The sugar amount is usually equal to the amount of juice—one cup of juice for every one cup of sugar.) Add four times the amount of water as juice. (One cup of juice should be added for every four cups of cold water.) Stir and taste. Add more water or sugar if needed. Put an ice cube in each child's glass and let the children taste.

Lacy Cupcakes

Make chocolate cupcakes from a boxed cake mix or your favorite recipe. Each child should place the lacy part of a doily over the top of a cooled cupcake and sprinkle powdered sugar over it. If you have a sifter, they might like sifting the sugar. Lift the doily straight up and look at the "Lacy" cupcake.

Lettuce Roll-Ups

You will need a large, clean, dry piece of lettuce for each child, dull knives for spreading, paper plates, and various spreads. (They should be reasonably soft so, when spreading, the children do not tear the lettuce.) Cheese spreads, peanut butter spreads, etc. are favorites. Children should spread a thin layer of their favorite spread on the lettuce, roll up the lettuce and eat it like a burrito.

146

"M" Vocabulary and Oral Expression

Introducing "M"

Introduce "m" words through conversation, illustrations, and questions. (What things can we measure? What do you know that will melt? Can you describe the color called maroon?)

Names		Animals	Foods	Opposites
Maria	Mary	mole	macaroni	mother—father
Martin	Mike	mouse	macaroon	morning—evening
Mickey	Molly	monkey	melon	men—women
Marcia	Margo	moose	muffin	man—woman
Marsha	May	mule	mushroom	miss—hit
Megan	Marie	muskrat	mustard	
Mimi	Mitzi		milk	**Homonyms**
Mark	Matthew		mayonnaise	meat—meet
Martha	Marty		marshmallows	made—maid
Michelle	Mac			mail—male
Morgan	Melissa			marry—merry—Mary
Margaret	Marjorie			

"M" Objects

Ask, "Can you tell me about any of the following things?" (Make a note of those things that no one can describe and provide pictures at a later date.)

marsh	microscope	magazine	map
money	meadow	magician	matches
mold	mustache	mattress	moon
magnet	medals	moss	mug

Tongue Twisters

- Ask the children to repeat in unison after you. Then ask if anyone would like to try to say a tongue twister as fast as possible alone.

  Mitzi made many muffins.   *Mark marched to the merry music.*
  The magician's magic is a mystery.   *Mike married Mary Monday.*
  Martin made a monster mask.   *Many men mowed the meadow.*

- Now ask students to add one or more "m" words to the following to make tongue twisters:

  Molly missed...
  Marcia made...
  Micky measured...
  Marcia Mouse mixed...
  In March Morgan met...
  Margaret moved...

- Tell the children to answer "yes" or "no" to these questions and to explain why they answered as they did.

  Can a magazine march?   *Can you mow money?*
  Is mud messy?   *Does a marble have a mustache?*
  Do magicians do magic?   *Can you march to music?*
  Do musicians play melodies?   *Would you expect to see moss in a market?*

"M" Art and Activities

Use Your Senses

Sense of Touch and Smell:
1. Duplicate the letter "M" on page 145.
2. Cover it with glue. Sprinkle with dried or fresh mint leaves, marjoram, or dry mustard.
3. Have students close their eyes, then feel and smell the page.

Sense of Taste
Have an "m" tasting day in the class. Students can taste "m" foods such as maple syrup, melons, molasses, and macaroons.

Sense of Hearing
Sing a melody. See if the children can sing it back to you.

Sense of Sight
Give children opportunities to use a microscope and magnifying glass to see how these things change their ability to see objects. Play, "I Spy." Items placed around the room might include money, a map, mittens, and a mug.

Singing Games

Play a game of Musical Chairs with your class.
Sing and act out songs such as *Here We Go 'Round the Mulberry Bush.*

Measuring

Read aloud *Inch by Inch*, by Leo Lionni (Knopf Books for Young Readers, 2010).

Have a table set up with as many items used in measuring as possible. (You may want to include a stopwatch, a clock, wet and dry measuring cups, spoons, a calendar, a ruler, scales, thermometers for air and body temperature, a bike speedometer, a yard stick, and measuring tape.)

Ask what each thing is used to measure. Give children an opportunity to use as many items as possible.

If you have enough rulers for every child to have one, they can use them to have a "measurement hunt." If you do not, duplicate the pattern on page 106, cut out and have children find items that are bigger than 6 inches, smaller than 6 inches, about 2 inches long, etc.

Mitten Match

Duplicate the mitten patterns on page 151, one per child. Tell them to decorate and color the mittens exactly the same. (Have some to illustrate.) They should then cut out the mittens and give one to you. They hide their eyes while you place one mitten from each pair in an odd place around the room. They hunt for their own matching mitten. Exchange mittens and play again. Some children may enjoy a turn doing the "hiding."

Mitten Patterns

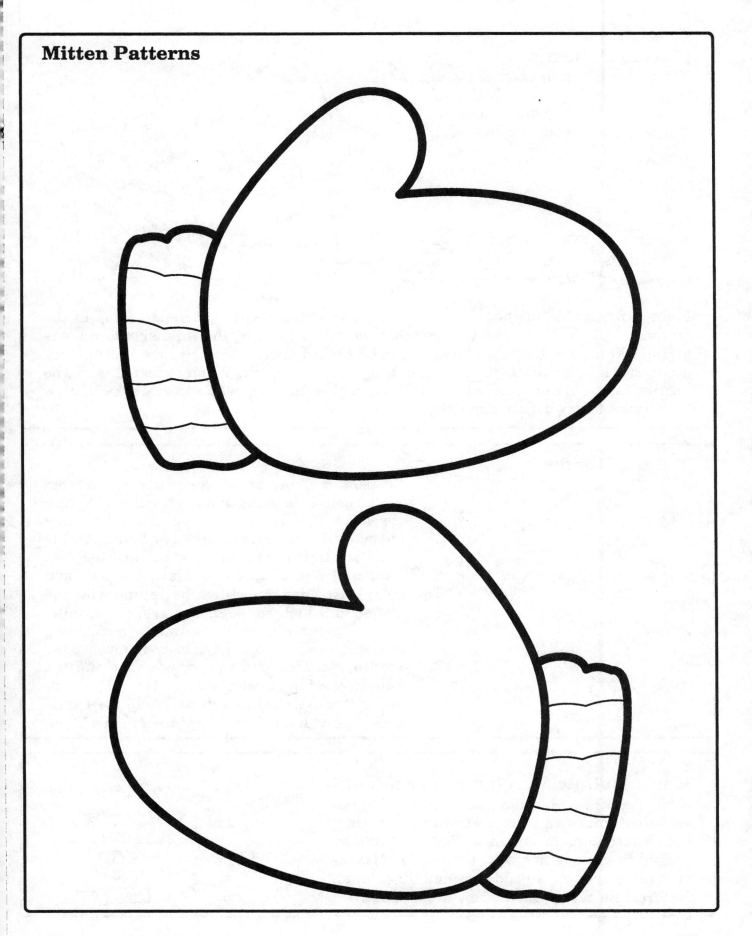

Marble Painting

You will need: a flat box as big as your paper with a lid
bag of marbles
posterpaints
paper

Place paper inside the box. Drip several colors of paint onto the paper. Drop in the marbles. Put the lid on the box. Holding the lid on the box, the child should roll the marbles around in the box. It should not be turned upside down. He may set the box down and lift the lid to see how the design is developing. When satisfied with the results, the child can remove the marbles and place in soapy water to be washed. Allow the picture to dry before displaying.

Make a Mobile

Suspend a string across a section of the room high enough to hang mobiles without hitting the head of your tallest child. Tie interesting shaped twigs with dental floss or fishing tackle and hang from the string. (You can also use coat hangers.) Ask children to draw, cut out, and color both sides of pictures beginning with the "m" sound, such as magnet, mask, meal, milk, money, mountain, men, mermaid, mop, mug, mittens, market, monkey, mouse, mushroom, muffin, etc. Then use a paper punch to punch a hole in the top of each picture, thread yarn or string through the hole (an adult will need to tie a knot), and hang from one of the twig mobiles.

Marshmallow Men (moose or mice)

Have bags of regular and miniature marshmallows, toothpicks and clean scissors for cutting. Let children create marshmallow creatures by joining them together with toothpicks. Marshmallows can be cut to add ears and other small features. Be sure to have a few extra to eat!

Making Music

Make some musical instruments using the following directions.

Sandpaper Blocks
Attach sandpaper to one side of two wooden blocks. Rub together in time to the music.

Rhythm Sticks
Use pairs of wooden toys, unsharpened pencils, dowels, or wooden spoons. Strike together in time to the music.

Maracas
Fill a margarine tub, plastic bottle, or bandage box with seeds, pebbles, rice, or buttons. Make sure the lid is secured and shake in time to the music.

Tambourine
Use two paper plates or aluminum pie pans. Decorate if you wish. Punch holes around the edges of the pans or plates. Place dried beans or seeds on one plate. Put the other plate face-down on top of it. With yarn or ribbon, sew the two objects together. Shake or hit with knuckles in time to the music.

Drum
See page 51 for directions to make a drum.

Memory Games

- Put five items on a tray and have children look at them without talking. Have them turn around and remove one thing. Let children turn back around to look at the tray and see who can remember which thing is missing.
- Show three things students are to bring up to the circle (crayon, sheet of paper, scissors). Do not talk. Put the items behind your back. See how many can remember to bring up the correct items.
- Give a verbal order to do three things (stand up, turn around, put your left hand on top of your head). Then increase the number of commands until no one can do all of them.

Money

Use transparent tape to attach sets of coins to small cards. Make two sets that are alike. Lay them out on a table and ask children to match the sets of coins that are alike.

Bring in rolls of coins so that each child can have one of each (penny, nickel, dime, quarter). Ask them to hold up the correct coin as you describe it. Then give directions such as: "Hold up the coin that is worth five cents. Show me the coin we call a dime. Hold up the largest sized coin in front of you. Who knows what we call it? How much is it worth?" If your children seem very aware of coin values, you can show them a dollar bill and discuss the value.

Magnets

Have a number of magnets and objects on a table. Let children experiment to see which objects the magnets will pick up. Make a picture chart to show which things magnets will pick up and which things they will not.

154

"M" Food

Mystery Muffins

You can make these at home and let each child discover what is hidden in the muffin or make with the children and let them put in the mystery ingredient.

Use a boxed muffin mix or your favorite recipe. Fill the muffin cups ⅓ full with batter. Then put in a food surprise (nuts, jelly, cream cheese, etc.). Cover with batter and bake according to the package directions.

Monster Cookies

Bring in large, round cookies or make a batch with the children. (For something quick and easy, let them roll out refrigerator dough and use large plastic lids as cutters.) Then let them design monster faces on the cookies using frosting tubes, candies, nuts, raisins, etc. Let them walk around and see all the creations before munching on their monsters.

Have a Munching Morning

Prepare or send a note home asking children to bring in snack foods that crunch when eaten (celery, dry cereal, carrots, etc.). Invite children to enjoy a "mid-morning munch". Have them try each of the different snack foods. Discuss the sound each snack makes when eaten.

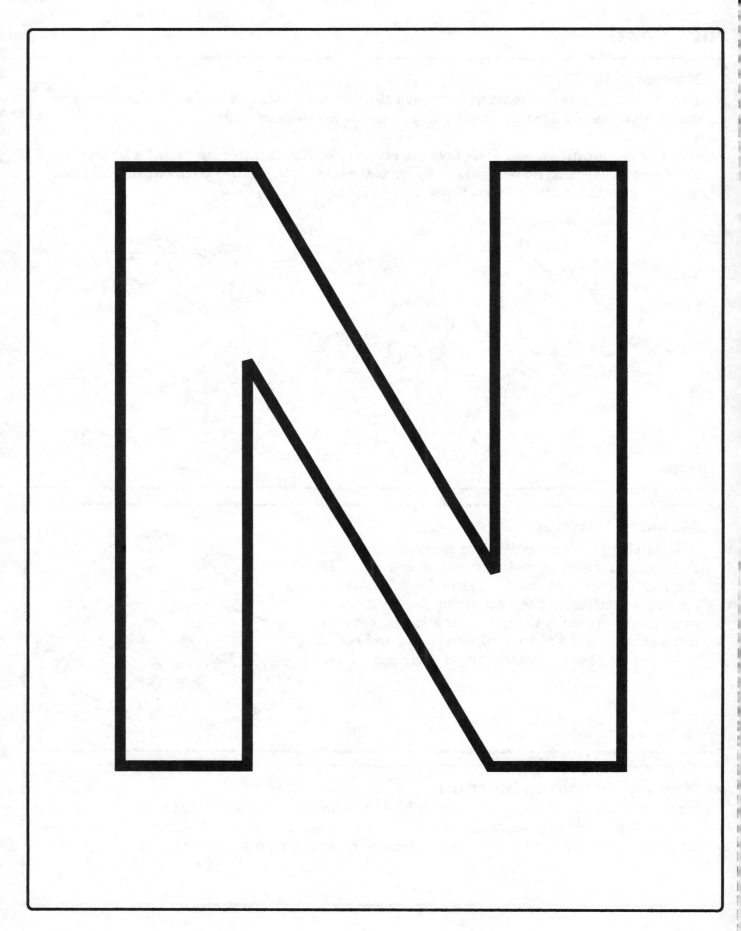

156

"N" Vocabulary and Oral Expression

Introducing "N"
Introduce "n" words through conversation, illustrations, and questions. (What time of day is noon? What is the noisiest place you have ever been? What does it mean if something is necessary?)

Names

Norma	Nicole
Natalie	Nellie
Noel	Neal
Nelson	Nicky
Nancy	Ned
Norman	

Opposites

night—day	now—later
naughty—good	near—far
narrow—wide	new—old
never—always	neat—messy
noisy—quiet	night—day

See page 124 for "kn" words that make the "n" sound.

"N" Word Meanings
Ask, "Can anyone tell me two meanings for the following words?"

nail	nursery
note	navy
nag	

"N" Numbers
Ask, "Can anyone come to the board and write one of the numbers I say?"

9	19	29
39	49	59
69	79	89
91	99	

"N" Objects

Ask, "Can you tell me about any of the following things?" (Make a note of those that no one can describe and provide pictures at a later date.)

net   nickel   nurse

napkin   newspaper   necklace

necktie   needle

Tongue Twisters

- Ask children to repeat in unison after you. Then ask if anyone would like to try to say a tongue twister alone as fast as possible.

  Nobody knew naughty Nellie's name.   *Nancy needs nine needles.*

  Nick notices his noisy neighbors.   *Ned knows nothing new.*

  Nora's nurse nibbles nectarines.   *Nel needs a new nickname.*

- Ask the children if they can add one or more "n" words to the following to make tongue twisters.

  Norma needs a new…

  Natalie's niece nodded to…

  Ned's neighbor knew…

  Nicholas's nickname is…

  Nellie nurse knows…

  Norman needed nineteen…

- Tell the children to answer "yes" or "no" to these questions and to explain why they answered as they did.

  Is a needle noisy?   *Could a necktie be navy?*

  Do neighbors have names?   *Do you nap at noon?*

  Could a niece wear a necklace?   *Do noses have numbers?*

  Can you nibble a nut?   *Do you think people read names*

  Might you see a nurse in a nursery?   *and notices in newspapers?*

"N" Activities

Number Activities
As an introduction to number activities, read aloud:
> *Chicka Chicka 1, 2, 3* by Bill Martin, Jr. and Michael Sampson. Simon & Schuster Books for Young Readers, 2004.
> *My First Counting Book* by Lilian Moore. Golden Books, 2001.

Hide and Seek

Make at least **two** copies of the numerals from the patterns on page 161. (Use the number one on the second sheet with the zero to form the numeral ten.) Cut out, mount each on a separate sheet of paper (1 to 10), and place in visible locations, but in unusual places around the room. Tell the children you have placed the numerals 1 through 10 around the room. When you say, "Go," they should begin to hunt and bring any they find to the table. When all have been found, select an "arranger" (perhaps the first one to find a numeral or someone who found more than one) to lay out the numerals on the table in correct order.

Variations: Hide numerals that continue beyond ten. If your class is small (or if you make small groups with a large class) hide enough numerals so that each child can look for his/her own set and arrange in correct order. Give each child his/her own envelope containing the numerals one through ten and some dried beans, buttons or markers. Ask them to arrange their numerals in correct order on a table or the floor and then make a pile of markers under each numeral to illustrate how many it represents.

Number Patterns

1 2 3 4

5 6 7

8 9 0

Number Game

Have all children but one sit on chairs in a circle. The person not sitting should stand in the middle. Beginning with the number one, each child should be given a number in consecutive order. (Some children who have difficulty remembering may need their number written on a sheet of paper.) The standing player calls out any two numbers and those two players try to exchange seats before the caller can sit in one of them. The person without a seat is the new caller.

Nicknames

Talk about nicknames. Ask children to share their nicknames and those of members of their families. Give everyone (or let each child select) a nickname for the day.

Find Your Name

Duplicate the letters on the first page of each section of this book and on pages 310 through 318. Make enough copies for each child to correctly spell out his first name. Ask students to look for the correct capital and lower case letters in their names on the pages, color, cut out, and arrange correctly in front of them. (Some children may need copies of their names and help with cutting.) When everyone is finished, pick up all the letters, ask children to hide their eyes, and place the letters all around the room. Then let children hunt for the letters to form their names.

Use Your Senses

Sense of Touch and Smell
1. Duplicate the letter "N" on page 156.
2. Cover it with glue. Sprinkle with nutmeg.
3. Have students close their eyes, then feel and smell the page.

Sense of Taste
Let students taste a nectarine. They can also try and compare different kinds of nuts.

Sense of Hearing
Have children turn their backs to you. Call each child's name softly. The child should say, "I hear you." Then softly say "n" numbers (9, 19, 29, etc.) to this child and ask him to repeat them. Everyone else should be very quiet.

Sense of Sight
Play "I Spy." Items around the room might include a notebook, numbers, napkins, a necklace and a newspaper.

Form Your Name
Direct each child to roll out a long clay rope. Use your classroom clay, your favorite clay recipe, or the recipe on page 35. Ask students to break off sections of the clay rope and form the letters that spell their names. Some children may need name cards to copy.

Make a "Nifty Necklace"
Provide children with lengths of string and pasta, cereal "O"s, or candy with holes. Let them thread the items onto the string to make necklaces.

Variation: Use blunt needles to string miniature marshmallows and/or gum drops to make necklaces.

"N" Food

Number Sandwiches

Use a number cookie cutter or make your own pattern and cut two slices of bread into the shape of a number (the date, child's age, etc.). Let children fill with peanut butter. (See page 161 for number patterns.)

Name Cookies

Let children roll out and cut cookie dough or bring in large circular or rectangular cookies. Using pointed frosting tubes, children can print their names on the cooked, cooled cookies. Make name cards for very young children to copy. If you have a small group of children they might enjoy making a cookie for each letter of their names. Use letter cookie cutters or make your own patterns (using the first page of each section and those on pages 310 through 318).

Nachos

Buy some tortilla chips to dip in melted cheese for a snack. You can make your own chips by cutting flour tortillas into fourths and baking in a 350° oven for 12 minutes on an ungreased cookie sheet.

Nutty Nibbles

You will need: one 12-ounce bag of milk chocolate morsels
$\frac{1}{2}$ cup peanut butter
2 cups coarsely chopped unsalted dry roasted peanuts

Melt chocolate and peanut butter in top of double boiler. Add peanuts and stir. Drop by teaspoonfuls on a foil or wax paper lined flat pan. Refrigerate until firm.

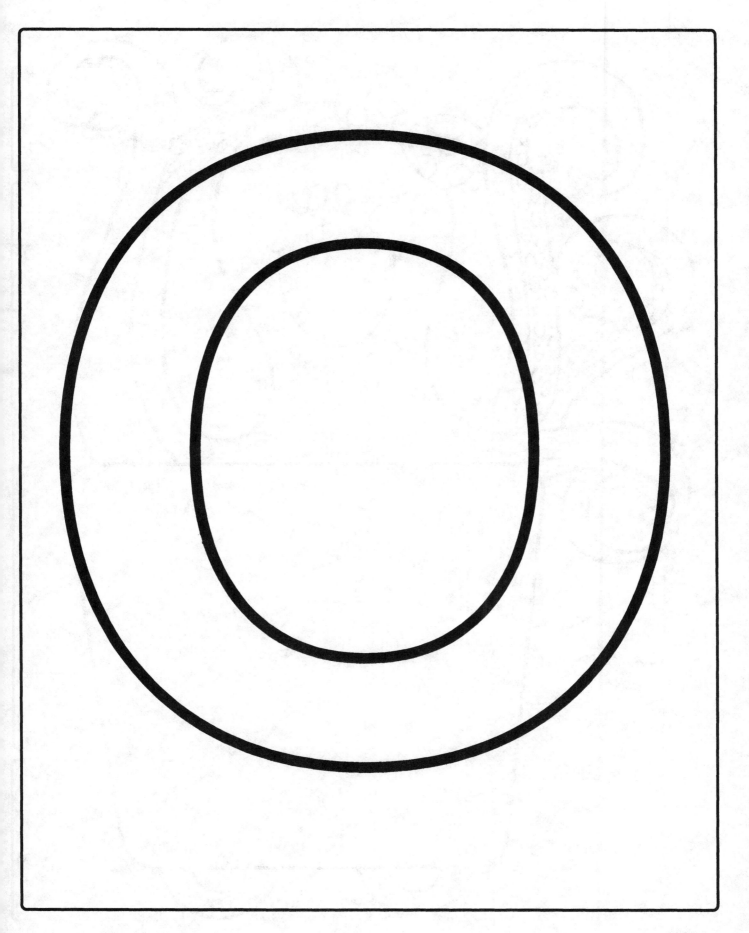

166

"O" Vocabulary and Oral Expression

Introducing "O"

Introduce "o" words through conversation, illustrations, and questions. (Why would a person want a pair of oars? Do you remember the last time you said, "Ouch!" What happened to make you say that? Does anyone in your family work in an office? Have you ever been there? Tell us about an office.)

Foods	Names	Animals	Opposites	Homonyms
olives	Otto	ocelot	on–off	owe–oh
onion	Olivia	opossum	old–new	or–ore–oar
orange	Opal	orangutan	out–in	
oatmeal	Oliver	otter	over–under	
	Otis	octopus	outdoors–indoors	
	Oscar	ox	open–shut–close	
	Ollie	ostrich		
	Oren	owl		

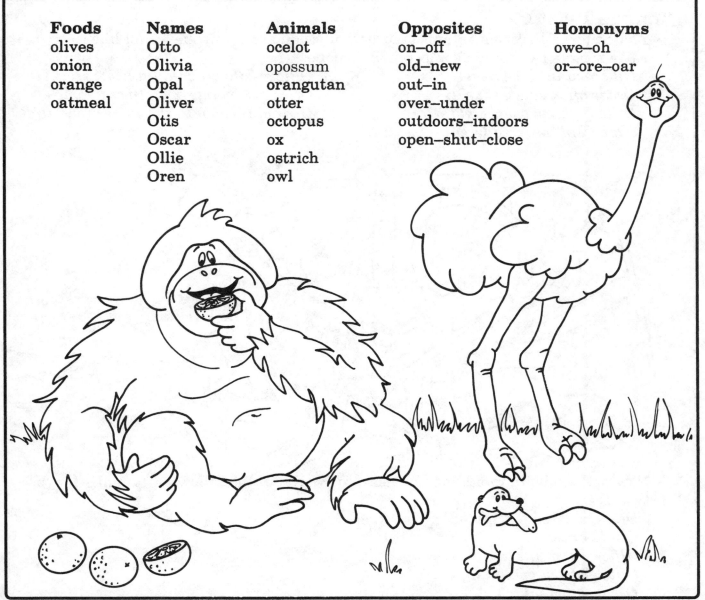

"O" Objects

Ask, "Can you tell me about any of the following things?" (Make a note of those things that no one can describe and provide pictures at a later date.)

ocean	oatmeal	oil
octopus	orchestra	olives

More "O" Questions

What kinds of officers do you know about?

What does a waitress mean when she asks, "May I take your order?"

What does an officer in the army mean when he says, "Now, that's an order!"

There are different kinds of operators. Do you know what any of them do?

Tongue Twisters

- Ask children to repeat in unison after you. Then ask if anyone would like to try to say a tongue twister as fast as possible alone.

    Oil oozed into the ocean.   *Officer Otto ordered the others out.*

    Oscar often eats oatmeal.   *Otis likes onions and olives in omelets.*

    Ollie Octopus owns eight oars.   *Opal plays oboe in the office orchestra.*

    "Open up!" ordered Oren.

- Now ask students to add one or more "o" words to the following to make tongue twisters.

    Otto Ox asked for another...

    Olivia orders...

    Officer Otis eats...

    Ollie Ostrich goes in and ...

    Oscar Otter said, "..."

    Oren Owl's oars fell...

- Tell the children to answer "yes" or "no" to these questions and to explain why they answered as they did.

    Would an ox play in an orchestra?   *Could you own an oboe?*

    Could an otter have an operation?   *Is on the opposite of off?*

    Could an office eat an orange?   *Can an owl live outdoors?*

"O" Activities

Use Your Senses

Sense of Touch and Smell
1. Duplicate the letter "O" on page 165.
2. Cover with glue. Sprinkle with oregano, orange gelatin powder, or onion salt.
3. Have students close their eyes, then feel and smell the page.

Sense of Taste
Let students taste several different types of oranges and compare their tastes. You may also have them try okra and types of olives.

Sense of Hearing
Ask children to close their eyes and listen carefully as you read the tongue twisters from page 168 aloud. Ask them to count how many "o" words they hear in each one. Have children work with partners to come up with silly sentences using as many "o" words as possible. Allow them to share their sentences with the class.

Sense of Sight
Play "I Spy." Items around the room might include an orange, pictures of an owl, an octopus, and an otter.

Obstacle Course
Make a simple, safe obstacle course in your classroom or outside. Include things that children must go around, under and over. (They can climb up and down a low step ladder, go under a table, around chairs, etc.) After everyone completes the course several times, you may wish to time each student and see who can go through the course in the shortest time without knocking anything over. Use as many "o" words as possible when giving instructions (over, on, out, open, off, outside, etc.).

Opposites

As an introduction to opposites activities, read aloud:

Exactly the Opposite, by Tana Hoban. Greenwillow Books, 1997.
Big Dog…Little Dog, by P.D. Eastman. Random House Books for Young Readers, 2003.
Eric Carle's Opposites, by Eric Carle. Grosset & Dunlap, 2007.

Play a game of "Opposite Toss." Have children stand in a circle. Say a word aloud and toss a ball to someone in the circle. That person should catch the ball and say a word that is the opposite. Then, that person should say a new word and toss the ball to another person, and so on.

Old–New

If it is spring, take a walk outside and look for old and new things in nature.

Old	New
leaves	leaves
bark	buds
trees	blossoms
nests	plants (shoots)

Variation—place some "new" things around the classroom and ask the children to take a look around the room for the old and new things.

Duplicate page 171 so each child has his own copy. Ask them to cut out the cards and match the opposites by putting them side by side. You may wish to have some blank cards so that some children can make more "opposite" cards.

Opposite Cards

Use these cards with the activity on page 170.

hard

cold

empty

full

hot

soft

big

small

Orange Day

Ask students to wear and/or bring something to school that is orange.

Read aloud *The Big Orange Splot*, by Daniel Manus. Pinkwater Hastings House, 1977.

Scoop out orange halves and fill the peel with orange sherbet. Let students eat the sherbet along with the removed orange sections at snacktime. They can also drink orangeade or juice. Give bite-size samples of other fruits and vegetables that are colored orange (tangerine, squash, apricot, carrot, pumpkin, peach, cantaloupe).

Let the children experiment with blending red and yellow to make orange by adding drops of food coloring into water and stirring. Give more opportunities to combine red and yellow by using crayons and water colors to make orange objects.

Add red and yellow food coloring to white frosting until it is orange. Spread on large flat or round cookies. Use candies, nuts, and/or raisins to make pumpkin faces or oranges with faces.

Orange Pompander Ball

Give each child a firm, ripe orange. Demonstrate how to poke holes all over the skin of the fruit. A sturdy toothpick will work. Direct them to push a whole clove into each hole, keeping the cloves as close as possible so the entire orange is covered. Insert a ribbon in the top with a large nail or tack or tie a ribbon around the entire orange. Hang it in a dry, cool place for two to three weeks. This can be given as a gift and hung in a closet or placed in a drawer. The scent will last for a long time.

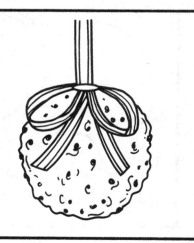

Octopus Art Activity

Give each child a copy of the octopus pattern below to color or let them draw their own. As children learn "o" words, they can draw a picture of each object and place it at the end of an octopus tentacle. The octopuses can be put on a blackboard that has been colored or decorated to look like the **ocean**.

Owls
Read *Owl Moon*, by Jane Yolen. Philomel Books, 1987.

Make Open-faced, Oval, Owl Sandwiches.

You will need:
- bread
- cream cheese
- spreaders
- raisins and/or grapes
- food coloring

Cut the bread into oval shapes. Use food coloring to make the cheese tan or brown. Direct the children to spread the cheese on the ovals and design an owl face by using grapes, raisins or shapes cut from the excess bread.

Make a Paper Plate Owl

Give each child an inexpensive paper plate to flatten. Duplicate the patterns on the next page and give a copy to each child. Direct the children to color the paper plates, color and cut out the patterns and glue them on the paper plates as illustrated.

Owl Patterns
Follow the directions on the preceding page to complete the paper plate owl.

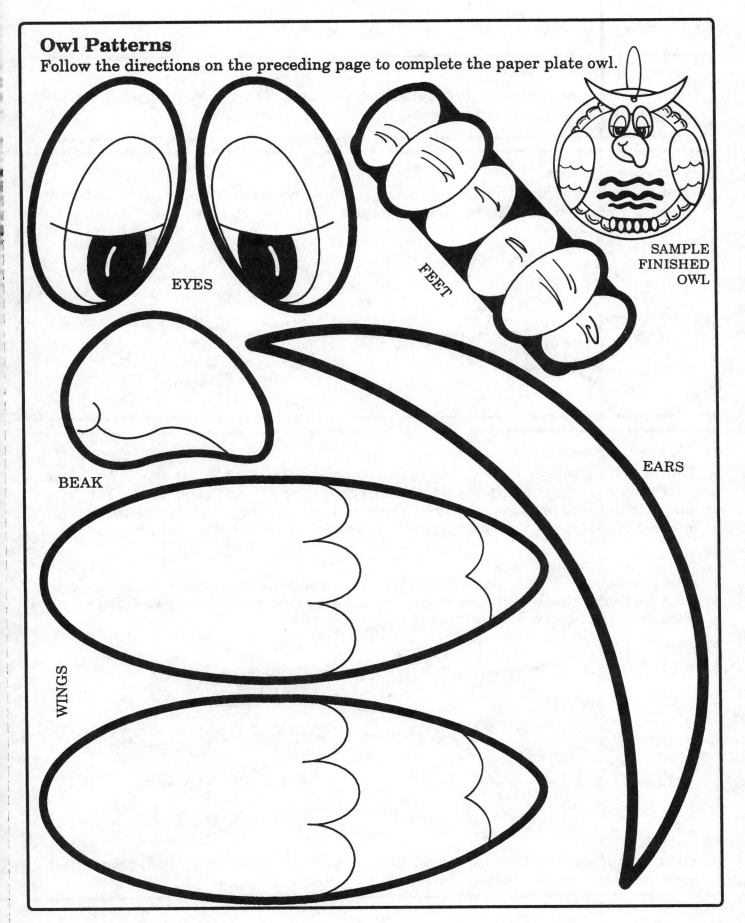

EYES

FEET

SAMPLE
FINISHED
OWL

BEAK

EARS

WINGS

"O" Foods

Orange Juice
Give children the opportunity to make fresh-squeezed orange juice from an electric or hand squeezer.

Orange Frosty
Make an "orange frosty" by adding a scoop of orange sherbet to 8 ounces of milk. Mix in a blender and pour into glasses for students to taste.

Octopus Sandwich
Cut bread slices into circles. Have children spread circles with the topping of their choice, such as peanut butter, jelly, cheese, orange butter (recipe below), etc. Let them add raisins, nuts or grapes for eyes. Have each student count and place the correct number of carrot and celery strips around the edge of his bread for the octopus legs.

Variation—Octopus Snack
Use an oatmeal cookie as the body. Spread with orange frosting (made by the children) with food coloring added. Use carrot strips or celery stuffed with orange-colored cream cheese for the legs for a truly "orange octopus."

Orange Butter: Mix 1 tablespoon confectioners' sugar, ¼ teaspoon grated orange peel with 4 tablespoons of whipped butter.

176

Oatmeal

Oatmeal Play

Spread dry oatmeal on cookie sheets. Ask children to use their fingers and practice forming the letter "o" in the oatmeal. Use dry oatmeal like sand for other play and finger drawing activities. It can be collected after students have finished with it and used again. Matchbox-size cars and trucks work well for this activity.

Mix a small amount of water with oatmeal until it has a consistency that will hold a shape. Children can mold it into forms (the letter "O," for example) or spread it on their drawings to give each one a three-dimensional look. Allow the drawings to air dry when students have finished sculpting.

Oatmeal Cooking

Serve bowls of cooked oatmeal and let children experiment with different toppings, such as brown sugar, raisins, nuts, cut up fruits (apples, bananas, etc.), syrups, honey, etc.

Make oatmeal cookies, bread, muffins or bars.

Oatmeal Cookies

You will need:
- 1 cup shortening
- 1½ cups brown sugar
- 2 eggs
- ½ cup milk
- ¼ teaspoon soda
- 2 teaspoons baking powder
- 1 teaspoon salt
- 1 teaspoon cinnamon
- ¼ teaspoon nutmeg
- 3 cups quick-cooking rolled oats
- ¾ cup chopped nuts

Cream the first three ingredients until light and fluffy. Stir in milk. Sift dry ingredients together and add to creamed mixture. Drop batter from a tablespoon two inches apart onto a greased cookie sheet. Bake at 400° for 8 minutes. Cool slightly before removing from pan.

178

"P" Vocabulary and Oral Expression

Introducing "P"

Introduce "p" words through conversation, illustrations, and questions. (Do you see some things around the room that are made of plastic? Can you tell me something about your pet? Why does a farmer use a plow?)

Names

Pam   Patty
Paula   Perry
Peggy   Polly
Paul   Penny
Peter   Penelope

Foods

peanut   parsnips
pancake   peach
plum   pecan
pizza   pickle
pie   popcorn
pork   potato
pumpkin   pepper
prune

Animals

penguin
pig
pigeon
polar bear
puppy
porpoise
partridge
porcupine
parrot

Careers

pilot
plumber
poet
police officer
postal worker

Colors

pink
purple

Homonyms

pair–pare–pear
peace–piece
plane–plain
peek–peak
pour–poor
pail–pale
pane–pain
paws–pause
peal–peel
pray–prey

"P" Objects

Ask, "Can you tell me about any of the following things?" (Make a note of those things that no one can describe and provide pictures at a later date.)

palace   pasture   patio   pansy
parachute   path   pliers   patch
pattern   pirate   platform   plug
puppet   pearls   pitchfork   pole
pebble   pond

Tongue Twisters

- Ask children to repeat in unison after you. Then ask if anyone would like to try to say a tongue twister as fast as possible alone.

  Peter Penguin paddled past Patsy.   *Peggy Pig preferred peas.*
  Penny Pigeon pecked peppermints.   *Peter peeled Paula's pears.*
  Paul passed pencils, pens, and paper. *Please pick the plump purple plums.*

- Ask the children if they can add one or more "p" words to the following to make tongue twisters:

  Penny poured...
  Polly Porpoise...
  Pam patted...
  Perry Puppy...
  Prissy's popcorn...
  Preston played...

- Tell the children to answer "yes" or "no" to these questions and to explain why they answered as they did.

  Can a package paddle?   *Could you paint a playpen?*
  Might someone bring pickles to a picnic?   *Can you pour from a pitcher?*
  Could you and a friend polka?   *Is it possible for a puzzle to pedal?*
  Can a pond be polite?   *Could a policeman be patient?*

"P" Art and Activities

Use Your Senses

Sense of Touch and Smell:
1. Duplicate the letter "P" on page 178.
2. Cover it with glue. Sprinkle with pepper, paprika, pine needles or parsley.
3. Have students close their eyes, then feel and smell the page.

Sense of Taste
Let students taste bite-sized bits of plums, peaches, pears, and pineapples. Discuss and compare the flavors. Taste peppermint candies.

Sense of Hearing
Listen to polka music. Listen to a "p" poem and have students learn part or all of it by rote. A good poem is "Pumberley Pott's Unpredictable Niece," from *The Random House Book of Poetry for Children,* selected by Jack Prelutsky (Random House, 1983).

Sense of Sight
Play, "I Spy." Items around the room might include a pail, pen, paper, paste, pillow, pencil and plant.

Have a "P" Picnic
Spread blankets on the floor of the classroom or outside if good weather and an appropriate place is available. Enjoy "p" foods on paper plates and in paper cups. You may wish to include pineapple juice, peanut butter, peas from the pod, potato chips or sticks, and pumpkin pie.

Popcorn Play

Have a "popcorn pop." Lay out large, clean sheets and ask children to sit on the edges. They must remain in their places. Place an electric popper without the lid in the center of the sheet. Pop the corn and watch it fly into the air. All that falls on the clean sheets may be eaten. All that goes onto the floor may be counted, glued on heavy paper in the shape of the letter "p," and/or put outside for the birds. For safety reasons, it is important that children not move from their seated positions until the hot popper has been removed.

Make Popcorn Piggies

You will need: 5 quarts of popped corn
½ cup light corn syrup
2 cups sugar
1 teaspoon vanilla
½ teaspoon salt
1 teaspoon vinegar
gumdrops and/or candy corn

Butter the bottom and sides of a saucepan. Combine the sugar, water, salt, syrup, and vinegar. Cook until the mixture reaches the hard ball stage and then stir in vanilla. Pour the mixture over the popped corn and mix well. Have children butter their hands. Give each one ¼ cup of the corn mixture and have them shape it into a ball. Add gumdrops and candy corn for eyes and legs. Curl a thin strip of licorice for a tail. Cut triangles from gumdrops for ears.

Pudding Painting

Cook pudding according to package directions and then cool. Let children finger paint on plastic or paper plates. They can eat their art or allow it to dry. If the finger painting is done on paper, it must dry completely before it can be displayed.

Puppets

Give children a variety of materials to use to make puppets. (Have a few completed or draw examples on blackboard to give them some ideas.) They can use the completed puppets to act out familiar stories and/or for free play.

Suitable materials include tongue depressors, ice cream sticks, old socks, mittens, paper plates and small paper bags, material scraps, buttons, yarn and colored paper.

Picture Puzzles

You will need: one 8" x 10" sheet of cardboard or poster board for each child (flexible enough for a child to cut)
full-page pictures from children's magazines
glue

Have each child glue one picture on the cardboard and trim off any extra. When the glue is dry, the board may be cut into 4 to 6 puzzle pieces. Each child can put his puzzle pieces into an envelope for exchange with other students.

Purple Day

Ask children to wear or bring something to class that is purple. Show them the color lavender and discuss shades of purple.

Read aloud *The Purple Pussycat,* by Margaret Hillert (Modern Curriculum, 1981) and *A Picture for Harold's Room,* by Crockett Johnson (Harper and Row, 1960). (Harold draws with a purple crayon.)

Let the children make the color purple by giving them an opportunity to mix red and blue food coloring in water and by combining red and blue crayons and paints on paper. Have them draw purple pictures.

Make "purple cows" to drink. Give each child a glass of grape juice or grape soda. Add a scoop of vanilla ice cream. Children can then stir and drink.

Have a Pink Party

Have a pink party. Let children experiment by adding small amounts of red food coloring to white frosting to make pink. Let them frost cupcakes or cookies pink. Serve with pink lemonade or pink punch.

Pickle Activities

Make pickle people by giving each child a large pickle, toothpicks and soft food items to attach (raisins, etc.) to make body parts and features on his pickle. The final activity could be a pickle people party or picnic where children could share their creations and then eat them. (Keep in mind that some children do not like the taste of pickles.) The class could make and/or discuss how pickles are made. Taste various types of pickles (sweet, dill, kosher, etc.).

Parachute Play

Many school physical education departments have parachutes, but if one is not available, large sheets or other lightweight material can be sewn together to use instead.

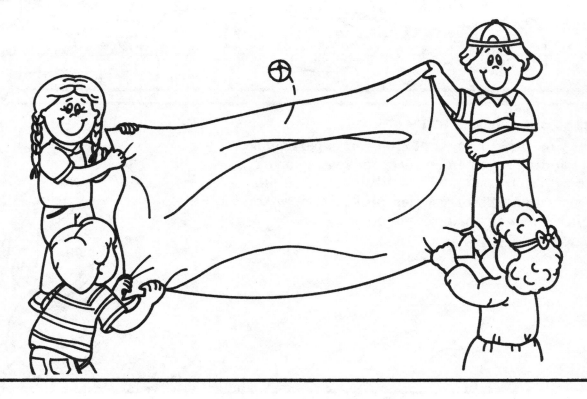

Play "What's in Polly Penguin's Purse?"

Use a large, soft-sided purse. Fill it with items that have a distinctive shape or feel (such as glasses, a tissue pack, a pencil, a pen, a safety pin, a comb, lipstick, a spiral note pad, keys, a hairbrush, a pack of gum, loose coins, etc.) Have children sit in a circle and pass the purse. Each one feels the contents from the outside of the purse to see if they can name one item inside. If correct, the teacher removes the item. The game is played until all items are gone. Variations: Each child must not only identify an object, but must give the beginning sound and/or letter for that object. Only items with names that begin with the letter "p" will be placed in the purse (pencils, pins, pens, paper, peppermint stick, popcorn, a pear, pennies, paste, pad, pearls, etc.).

Pretzel and Pasta Pictures

Ask children to draw "p" objects. Have various shapes of pretzels and pasta available. Have children use white glue to glue the pasta and/or the pretzels onto their papers on the lines of their drawings. Students can also use this procedure to make pretzel or pasta people. Be sure to put aside a few pretzels for snacking.

Potato Races

Divide the class into two or more teams. Give the first person in each team a potato and a spoon. Draw start and finish lines. When the signal is given, the first person must move as quickly as possible from the start line to finish line, carrying the potato on the spoon. If it is dropped, the player must go back to the start again. The spoon and potato are then passed to the next player who must repeat the run from start to finish. The first team to have all players complete the race is the winner.

Alternate Race: Each player must get down on his hands and knees and roll a potato to the finish line with his nose. The player may then pick up the potato and run back to the start line and give it to the next player in line on the team. Play continues until all have had a turn. Give potato chips or sticks to all for being "perfect potato players."

Potato Printing

Slice large potatoes in half. Have each child make a design on the cut side by digging out sections of the potato with a plastic knife or other object (dangerous sharp objects are not necessary). Let students print their designs by pressing the potatoes onto an ink pad or several layers of paper towels soaked with tempera paint. They can then press the potatoes onto sheets of paper. The completed sheets can be displayed and also make interesting wrapping paper.

188

Fun with Peanuts

Hide peanuts in the shell around the room before children arrive for class. Explain that they will be "peanut hunting," and let them know how much time they will have to hunt. Give a signal for everyone to begin hunting, and after the appropriate time (or after all the peanuts have been found), give the signal for them to stop, return to their seats and count the number of peanuts they found. Give some peanut butter–filled candy to the winner and to each of the other children for being good players.

Make Peanut Butter

Ask the children to shell their peanuts from the hunt and to put them in a one-cup measuring cup until it is full. Allow the students to eat any that remain. Put the cup of peanuts in an electric blender with two tablespoons of corn oil. Grind. Continue to add small amounts of oil until the peanut butter is the consistency you prefer. Salt to taste. Have children spread on crackers for a snack.

Peanut Butter Play Dough

You will need: 2 cups non-fat powdered milk
2 cups peanut butter
1 cup honey

Mix the above ingredients until the above mixture forms a soft, pliable dough. If necessary, add more honey and powdered milk to get the correct consistency. Spoon some on each child's plate. Ask the children to form the letter "p" with their dough and then form a "p" person or animal. After completing, allow time for children to walk around and view each other's creations. It is best to eat the peanut butter art right away.

Polka Dots

Duplicate the pattern below for each child. Ask them to use crayons or markers to turn it into a Polka Dot Puppy. The finished puppies can be cut out for display on a bulletin board.

190

"P" Food

Polka Dot Cookies

Buy or make cookies that are large, round and flat. Have children frost and add flat round colored candies to create a polka dot effect.

Variation: With cookie cutters or homemade cardboard patterns, make cookies in the shapes of "p" animals (such as pigs, polar bears, penguins, puppies, etc.). Frost and add candies to make the animals polka dotted.

Pizza Party

Roll refrigerator biscuits flat and have various toppings available for children to add to make small pizzas (such as various cheeses including mozzarella and parmesan, tomato or pizza sauce, dried oregano, and meats and vegetables you think will appeal to your students). Cook a few at a time in a toaster oven if no large oven is available. Refer to the time and temperature that is recommended on the biscuit package when cooking your pizzas.

Variation: For larger individual pizzas, use English muffin halves. Since you are studying the letter "p," this might be a good opportunity to encourage students to taste other "p" foods.

192

193

"Q" Vocabulary and Oral Expression

Introducing "Q"
Introduce "q" words through conversation, illustrations and questions. What game does a quarterback play? Is it good for him to be quick? What things can you buy by the quart? When there is an earthquake, what happens? If someone asks you to quit, what do they want you to do? Which is money, a quilt or a quarter? What is the opposite of quiet? quick? quit?

"Q" Objects
Ask, "Can you tell me about any of the following things?" (Make a note of those things that no one can describe and provide pictures at a later date.)

queen	quilt	quarterback
quarter	quail	question mark
quarry	quartet	

Tongue Twisters

- Ask children to repeat in unison after you. Then ask if anyone would like to try to say a tongue twister as fast as possible alone.

  The queen quickly hid under the quilt.
  Quentin Duck quipped, "Quit Quacking!"
  The quartet of quails quivered and quaked.

- Tell the children to answer "yes" or "no" to these questions and to explain why they answered as they did.

  Could a quail ask a question? *Could you have a quart of quacks?*
  Could you quarrel with a queen? *Could a quilt give you a quarter?*

"Q" Activities

Use Your Senses

Sense of Hearing

Let your class listen to recordings of barbershop quartets. Ask four children to sing a song together. Ask the class why they would be called a quartet. (With more mature students, you might listen to or discuss solos, duets, trios, etc., for comparison.) Have a quiet listening time. Ask children to close their eyes and raise their hands if they hear any noise at all. Then have them describe it.

Sense of Sight

Discuss the meaning of the word *quadrangle*. Ask the children to look around the room for quadrangles and count the sides. Play "I Spy" using pictures placed around the room (including pictures of a queen, a quilt, a question mark, and a quarter).

Sense of Touch

Bring in a sample of quartz or quartz glass to feel and discuss. You may also have students talk about a queasy feeling.

Sense of Taste and Smell

Taste and smell quince jelly and a quiche. (If you have the facilities, children may enjoy making quiche in individual tart pans.)

Make a Quilt

Suggested Reading: *The Quilt Story,* by Tony Johnston and Tomie de Paola. G.P. Putnam's Sons, 1985; *The Quilt,* by Ann Jonas. Greenwillow, 1985.

Give children squares of paper at least 5"x 5" in size. Ask each student to design and draw his own patch. You may wish to give them a theme, such as shapes, flowers, favorite storybook character, animal, etc. Arrange the completed paper patches on a bulletin board to demonstrate how a quilt is put together.

Then give children squares of material. (Cut up old sheets work well.) You may wish to starch the material to give it more body. It is more difficult to draw on material, so tape each patch firmly to a work table. You can let children design their own patches or suggest themes. An alphabet quilt is a possibility, with each child doing a letter. These patches can be sewn on a machine. Perhaps a room mother or aid would do this job. The completed work can be attached to an old coverlet and displayed in the room or used in the housekeeping play area.

Variation: Send a note home explaining your quilt project. Ask each child to bring in a 5"x 5" square of material that has meaning to him, with or without a design (an old square from a baby blanket, for example).

Stitch a Quilt

Duplicate this page on heavy paper or glue duplicated sheets to thin cardboard. Punch out circles with a paper punch. Direct children to color the pictures. Give them large, blunt needles with yarn connected to "stitch" the quilt.

Questions

Read the book *National Geographic Little Kids First Big Book of Why*, by Amy Shields (National Geographic Books, 2011). This book answers many questions that children have, such as: Why do planes fly? Why is the sky blue? Why do bees make honey? After reading the book, ask children what other questions they have wondered about. Copy down their questions, answer some of them immediately if possible (other students may even be able to answer some) and find books to read aloud in the coming weeks that help answer their questions. Make a copy of the question mark on the right side of this page for each child. Ask them to trace and color it. Place the question marks on a bulletin board beside children's drawings showing their questions and answers.

Play "Quack, Quack"

Children sit in a circle around one child who is "it." That child sits in a chair blindfolded with an object under the chair to represent a duck's egg. The adult leader points to one child who goes to the chair, takes the egg, sits down placing the egg behind him, and quacks, trying to disguise his voice. The blindfolded child in the center removes the blindfold and has three guesses as to who has the egg. If correct, the two children exchange places.

Queens

Read the nursery rhyme *The Queen of Hearts*. Buy some unfilled tarts. Have children make instant pudding, fill the tart shells, and act out the nursery rhyme so everyone has an opportunity to be either the queen or the knave. Students may use the crown pattern (on page 200) and enjoy the tarts at snack time.

Discuss and/or read stories that have queens (Sleeping Beauty, Snow White, etc.). Also show pictures of real queens. Duplicate the crown on the following page and have various materials children can use to decorate their crown (paints, glitter, etc.). Send a note home a few days before this activity asking for old beads and jewelry that could be glued on the crowns. Let children wear their crowns for free play and to act out stories about queens. During the summer, collect and press some Queen Anne's lace so it will be available when you are presenting the letter Q. Discuss how it got its name.

A Queen's Crown

Duplicate a crown pattern for each child on heavy paper. Ask children to cut the patterns out (if they are able) and have an adult staple together. The size of the crowns will be such that they perch on students' heads rather than fitting around their heads. To complete, follow the directions on page 199.

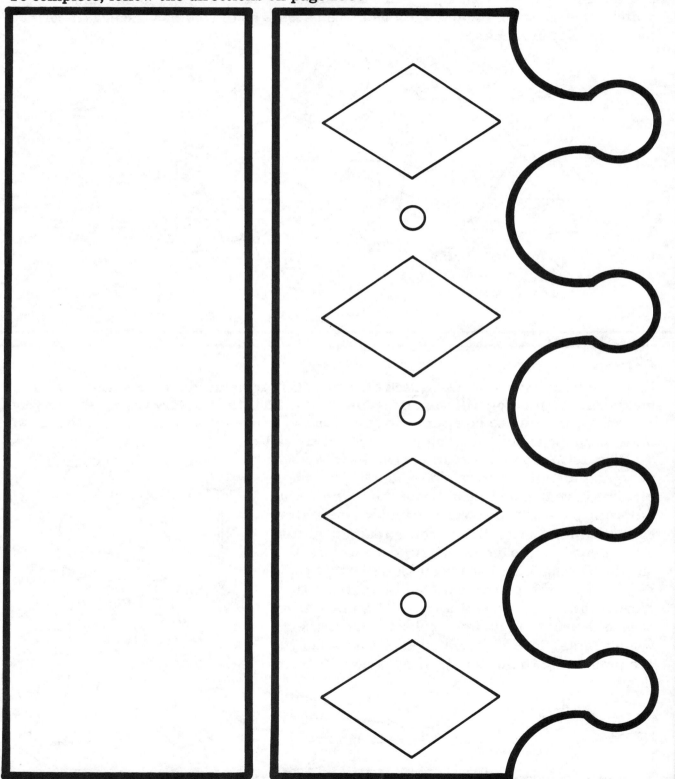

201

202

"R" Vocabulary and Oral Expression

Introducing "R"

Introduce "r" words through conversation, illustrations, and questions. (Can you repeat a nursery rhyme? Let's see how many things we can name that are round. What do you like to listen to on the radio?)

Names		Homonyms	Animals	Foods
Ralph	Rachel	reel—real	rabbit	raspberries
Robin	Ruby	role—roll	raccoon	raisins
Robert	Rochelle	ring—wring	rat	rice
Roberta	Rita	red—read	reindeer	rolls
Richard	Ronald	right—write	rhinoceros	rhubarb
Raymond	Ross	road—rode—rowed	rattlesnake	radishes
Rose	Russell		rooster	rutabaga
Ruth	Roger		Raven	

"R" Opposites

Ask students to tell the opposites of these "r" words:

rough	raw
rich	remember
reverse	return
rise	right

You may also give the following words and ask students to tell "r" words which are opposite of the words you name:

smooth	cooked
poor	forget
forward	take
fall	wrong (also "left")

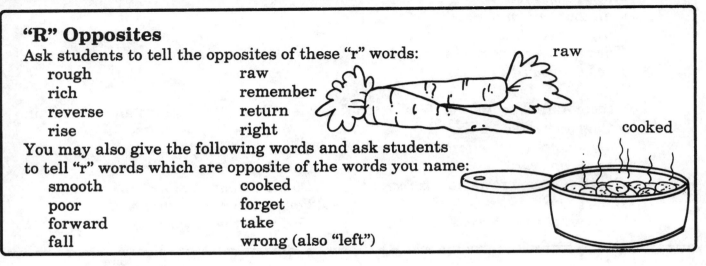

raw

cooked

"R" Objects

Ask, "Can you tell me about any of the following things?" (Make a note of those that no one can describe and provide pictures at a later date.)

rack	rake	rectangle	rocket
ranch	ribbon	rug	rainbow
razor	rifle	ruler	rope
rose	rubbish	root	rib
refrigerator	river	record	raft

Tongue Twisters

- Ask the children to repeat in unison after you. Then ask if anyone would like to try to say a tongue twister as fast as possible alone.

Ralph Rabbit ran around the ranch.　　　　*Robin Roberts remembers riddles.*
Roger Rat rode on the rim of the raft.　　　*Richard gave Rita a red ring.*
Ross is Russell Raccoon's relative.　　　　*Ruby ran a race in the rain.*
The ranger remembered the ripe raspberries.

- Ask the children if they can add one or more "r" words to the following to make tongue twisters.

Roberta raced...
Ruth raised red...
Run and return the...
Rita ruined the...
The repairman removed the...
Rochelle rowed in the...

- Tell the children to answer "yes" or "no" to the following questions and to explain why they answered as they did.

Can you see your reflection in a rock?　　*Can a rake run?*
Can a rag read?　　　　　　　　　　　*Could you ruin rice?*
Could someone remember a recipe?　　　*Does a ribbon rumble?*
Can a riddle be repeated?　　　　　　　*Would you rent a reindeer?*
Can a root be removed?　　　　　　　　*Can you ride on a rib?*

"R" Art and Activities

Rainbows

Read *A Rainbow of My Own*, by Don Freeman (Puffin, 1978) and *Elmer and the Rainbow*, by David McKee (Andersen Press USA, 2011).

Enjoy a fruity rainbow treat. Bring in fruits to represent each color of the rainbow (strawberries, cantaloupe, pineapple, kiwi, blueberries, grapes, etc.). Allow children to use the fruit to create an edible rainbow on a paper plate.

Make Rainbows

Fill a large glass jar with water. Be sure to place it so children can walk around it and see it from all sides. (This activity works best if the water is allowed to sit for a day.) Hold a bottle or dropper full of food coloring a few inches above the water and place a drop each of red, yellow, and blue food coloring into the water. Children can sit or walk around and watch the colors spread and blend in the water.

If you have a hose with a spray head, go out on a sunny day and make a fine mist spray. Have the children stand back and look for the rainbow.

Bring a prism in to class. Hold it up to the sunlight to show the reflected rainbow of colors.

Draw a rainbow with glue from a pointed bottle. Sprinkle with bands of colored rice (see directions on page 206 for coloring), pasta, or sand.

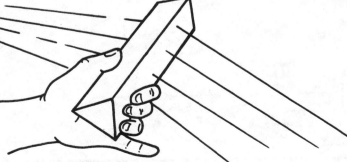

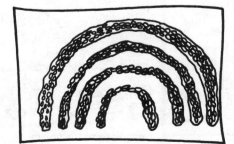

Rice Art

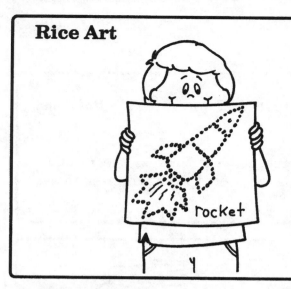

To dye rice, place a good quantity of rice in several containers. Add a cup of boiling water to each and two teaspoons of vinegar. Stir 15 drops of food coloring into each container, stir, and let rice sit for a few minutes. Drain and allow to dry in a paper-lined strainer.

You might begin the rice art activity by having the children form the letter "r" with glue and cover with colored rice. Try other "r" rice creations, such as rabbit, rocket, rug, rose, rain, rectangle and ring.

Rock Art

You will need:
- smooth rocks in all shapes and sizes
- disposable covers for work areas
- pencils, pens, markers
- poster or enamel paints
- paintbrushes
- varnish or shellac (optional)

Wash the rocks and allow them to dry for at least a day. Some children might like to practice designs on paper before they put them on their rocks. Direct children to cover all surfaces but the bottoms of the rocks with markers or paint. Allow the painted stones to dry overnight. If you wish the rocks to be shiny, apply a coat of thinned shellac or varnish to them when they are dry. The completed rocks can be given as gifts and/or used as paperweights.

Variation: Use acrylic paints and use an acrylic spray when dry.

Relay Races

Divide children into two or more teams. Have relay races involving "r" movements and/or materials. Let the students complete the following activities:

Running—Run to a line and then back to the starting line; run around a rug and back to starting line

Rope—Run and jump over a low rope and back to starting line

Roll—Roll a ball to a finish line. Pick up and run back to starting line.

Reindeer Race—Duplicate the antlers below onto heavy paper for each team. The runner for each team must hold them up to his head as he is running and then pass them to the next player when he is done.

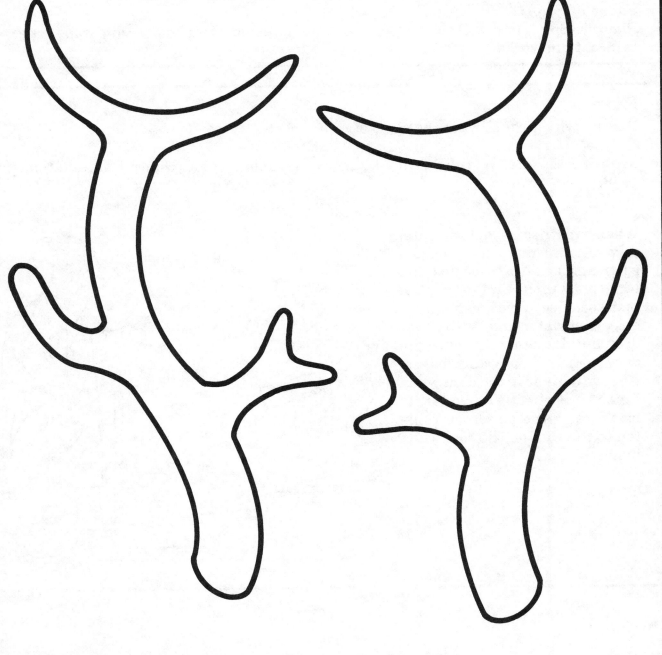

Additional races could be done using rocks, rice and red objects.

Use Your Senses

Sense of Touch
1. Duplicate the letter "R" on page 201.
2. Cover it with glue. Sprinkle with rice.
3. Have students close their eyes and then feel the page.

Sense of Taste
Let students sample rye bread, rice pudding, raspberry jam, or rhubarb sauce.

Sense of Hearing
Listen to music played on a recorder. Ask children to listen to pairs of words to see if they rhyme (such as run–fun and run–man). Then they can listen to pairs of words and tell which one starts with the "r" sound (as in rake–take and mug–rug).

Sense of Sight
Play, "I Spy." Items around the room might include ribbons, a rug, rope, rags, a raincoat and rocks.

Rain

Discuss why it rains, what the signs of rain are, etc.

Read *Will it Rain?* by Bill Martin Jr. and John Archambault (Henry Holt and Company, 1988).

When weather is appropriate, take a "rainy day walk." Take a ruler and use it to measure the length, width and depth of puddles. See if you can find a stream of water and let the children build a dam to reroute the water. Float boats and leaves. Be sure to remove the dam when finished. Collect rainwater to measure in the classroom. Listen to the rain on the roof when inside.

Red Day

Ask children to wear and/or bring something to class that is red.

Read aloud *The Little Red Caboose*, by Marian Potter (Golden Books, 2000) and *Red: Seeing Color All Around Us*, by Sarah L. Schuette (Capstone Press, 2006).

Provide children with construction paper, scissors, glue, and several magazines. Ask them to create collages made of red objects.

Let the class draw or paint red pictures. Make red robots from red modelling clay. For snack time, sample red foods such as apples, strawberries, tomatoes, radishes and red jam or jelly sandwiches. Make red gelatin in a large, flat pan. Cut out one large "R" and several small "r"s from the pan.

Play "Red Light, Green Light"

Using the patterns on page 210, have each child make his own set of lights which can be taken home for neighborhood play. Play outside whenever possible.

Rules: Children line up across the playground or room with toes on a line. A "traffic director" stands on a line facing them some distance away. The object of the students is to move toward and over the director's line. Children may walk when director holds up green, but must stop on red. Children that do not follow directions or that are caught walking on a red light go back to the starting line. The game is over when everyone has crossed the director's line. At that time a new director is chosen. (The new director could be the first to have crossed the line.)

Red Light, Green Light Patterns

STOP

GO

"R" Food

Rainbow Cupcakes

Make a yellow or white cake mix according to the directions on the box. Line or grease cupcake pans and fill as directed. Demonstrate how to add drops of food coloring to each unbaked cupcake. Use two knives and "cut" the colors into the batter rather than stirring them into it. A final swirl can be made on the batter top. Give each child an opportunity to color one cupcake. Bake according to package directions. If you wish to frost, rainbow frosting can be made in the same manner.

Ribbon Sandwiches

You will need: One or more loaves of uncut bread
three 8 oz. packages of cream cheese for each loaf of bread
food coloring

Make three horizontal cuts in the loaf of bread. Soften the packages of cream cheese. Add a different food coloring to each package. Spread one color cheese on each layer and reassemble the loaf. Cut a vertical slice for each child.

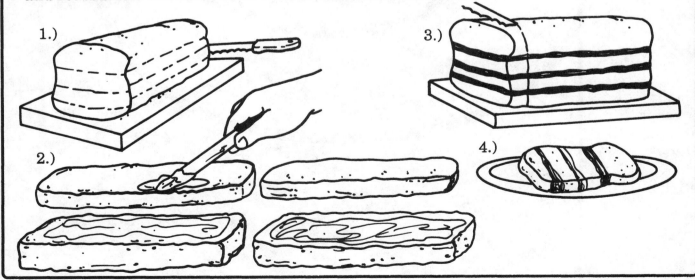

212

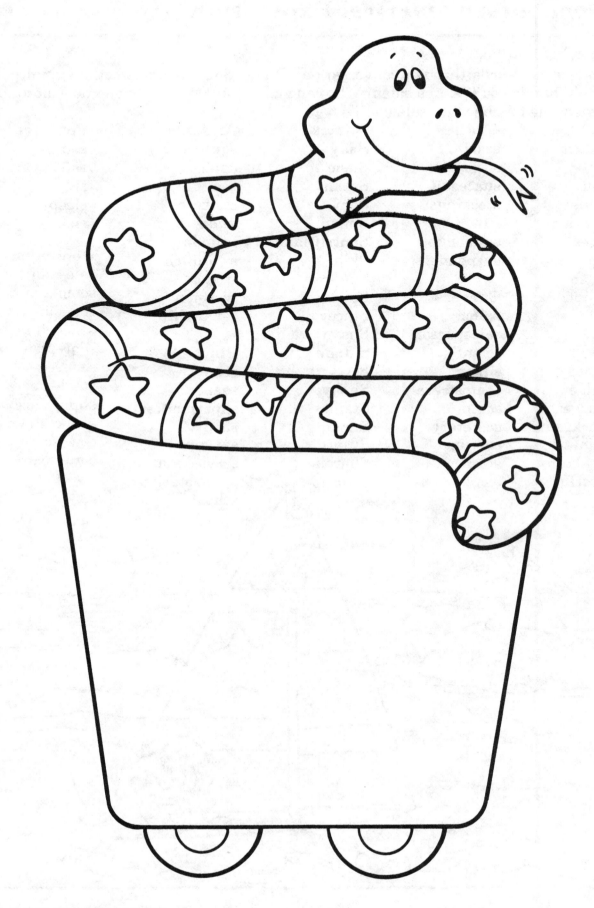

"S" Vocabulary and Oral Expression

Introducing "S"

Introduce "s" words through conversation, illustrations, demonstrations, and questions. (What do you like in a salad? Who can make a silly face? Do you know more than one meaning for the word sale [sail]?)

Foods	Clothes	Names	Animals	Feelings
spinach	scarf	Sally	squirrel	sad
salt	socks	Susie	snail	safe
sugar	spacesuit	Sarah	seal	silly
saltines	stockings	Sam	snake	sleepy
sandwich	suit	Simon	swan	sick
sauces	sunbonnet	Santa Claus	salmon	
soup	suspenders	Skip	swordfish	**Homonyms**
squash		Sandra	spider	sale–sail
scallion	**Careers**	Sandy	scorpion	seem–seam
scallops	sailor	Stacey	sea urchin	son–sun
salad	salesperson	Susan		sell–cell
stew	scientist	Sidney	**Places**	sent–scent–cent
seafood	singer	Scott	store	sea–see
sundae	seamstress	Shelly	seaport	steal–steel
sausage	sculptor	Stanley	supermarket	stair–stare
sauerkraut	secretary	Steve	shop	steak–stake
spaghetti	servant	Stuart	swamp	sew–so–sow
strawberry	soldier	Sharon	service station	sore–soar
spareribs			space station	
			school	

214

"S" Meanings

Encourage children to discuss the multiple meanings of the words below.

spring	stand	spade	spoke	sound
stick	soil	seed	sock	seal
stamp	saw	still	strain	stump
season	swell	sign	swallow	swing

"S" Objects

Ask, "Can you tell me about any of the following things?" (Make a note of those things that no one can describe and provide pictures at a later date.)

stapler	stem	strainer	submarine	sombrero
soccer	silo	scarecrow	scoreboard	scorpion
souvenir	sculpture	sailboat	sketch	sloth
schedule	smock	snorkle	saucer	sundial

"S" Questions

Tell children to answer "yes" or "no" to these questions and to explain why they answered as they did.

Can spaghetti scream?   Can sitters sew?
Can socks sip?   Can sewers smell?
Can a sled sneeze?   Can sandals separate?
Can skates squeak?   Can a sink squeeze?
Can scissors scratch?   Can a soda swallow?
Can spiders spin?   Can scarecrows ski?

Tongue Twisters

• Ask children to repeat in unison after you. Then ask if anyone would like to try to say a tongue twister as fast as possible alone.

Small Sammy seal swims sideways.   *Susie's sitter speaks softly.*
Sue slippery snake slides slowly.   *Six scary skeletons sing spooky songs.*
Seventy-seven silver stars sparkle.

• Now ask students to add one or more "s" words to the following to make tongue twisters:

Sally sews...
Simon squirrel scatters...
Smart Sarah saves...
Soft soap seems...
Susie salmon saw...
Sweet Stacey smells sauerkraut and ...
Sleeping Santa snores...
Sandy salamander...
Scott sings...

"S" Senses

Sense of Taste

• Categories of Taste

You will need: one paper plate with lines dividing it into three sections for each child

small samples of foods that are sweet, salty and sour (potato chips, saltines, pretzels, sugar cubes, soft candy, donut bits, grapefruit slices, sour cherries)

copies of the patterns below

glue

Ask children to color and cut out the salt shaker, sugar bowl, and lemon slice. Glue one picture to each section of the paper plate. Pass around samples of sweet, sour, and salty foods. Ask the children to place them on the section of the plate where they think they should go. When everything has been passed, discuss and let the children taste to see if they were correct.

• Seeds

Bring in various seeds for the children to taste, such as nuts, beans, peas, caraway, celery, etc. Discuss and compare the flavors and textures.

Sense of Smell

You will need: one blindfold for each child

materials with recognizable odors

        (spices, onion, peppermint, chocolate,

        scratch and sniff stickers, felt markers

        with fruit odors, etc.)

Children sit in a circle blindfolded. Pass one item under each child's nose. The children should not touch the item or talk. After everyone has smelled the object, one person at a time guesses what it is. The first person who is correct may pass the next item.

Sense of Touch

• Touch Box

You will need: a large box

small "s" objects (string, sock, sandpaper, straw, unwrapped bar

        of soap, spoon, ice cream scoop, skate, strainer)

Cut a hole in the side of the box just large enough for a child's hand. Fill the box with "s" objects. Children take turns closing their eyes, reaching in the box and trying to identify one of the objects by touch. Children making correct identifications may remove the objects. You can make a "sleeve" for this box by attaching the cuff of an old sock or mitten to the hole. This makes it nearly impossible to see the objects inside the box.

• Touching Board

You will need: a large flat board placed on a table or desktop

materials having textures that can be described with "s" words

        (Examples: **smooth**—satin, silk, suede

                sticky—taffy, rubber cement

                slippery—oil on a plastic plate or tray

                stiff—starched cloth)

Attach all materials firmly to the board. You may wish to blindfold children for this activity. Ask them to feel each item and to say an "s" word that describes the item.

• Letter S

Have children cover the letter "S" from page 212 with glue and then sprinkle with an "S" material (such as sand, sugar, salt, or sprinkles). Ask them to close their eyes and feel the letter by tracing it with their fingers.

Sense of Sight

• I Spy

This activity requires advance preparation that is done when children are out of the room. You may already have items that begin with the "s" sound that are in clear view (such as scissors, the sink, a smock, and the numerals 6 and 7). If not, put items in clear view of all the children. (These can include things like a square, soap, a skeleton, a sponge, straws, a spaceship, or a submarine.) Begin the game by saying, "I spy an 's' object that…" and give a clue to the object you have spied. The one who guesses correctly may then say, "I spy." You may need to whisper a suggestion for an object or a clue for some of the children.

Sense of Hearing

• Distinguishing Sounds

You will need: one copy of the listening board below for each child
nine large seeds or markers for each child
materials to make the sounds illustrated on the board
(two spoons, a ball, tissue paper, a bell or other small
hand-played musical instrument)

Duplicate the listening board below. (You may wish to glue the sheet on cardboard and laminate it.) Give one board and nine markers to each child. The sounds can be made by you or another adult, but they should be made out of the children's view. You can work behind a desk or screen or children can use their game boards with their backs to the person making the noises. There should be no talking or other noise. After all sounds have been done once, do them a second time. This time, the children may call out what they think they heard and remove each marker as they hear the sound for the second time.

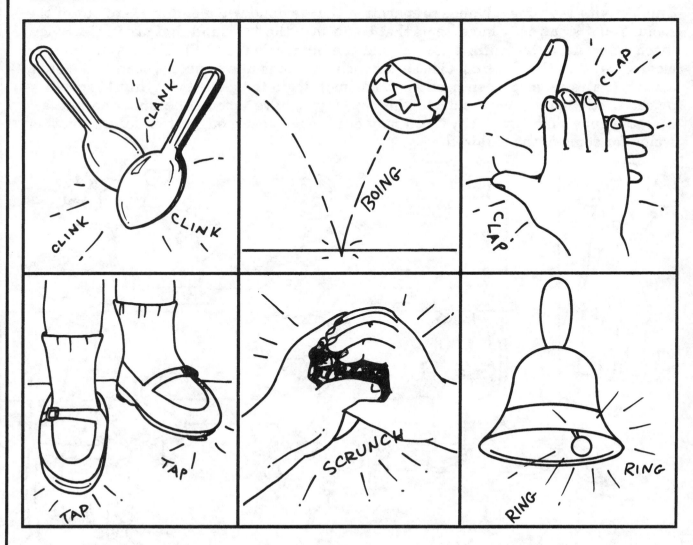

"S" Art

Snow Pictures

You will need:
- 1 cup soap flakes
- 2 cups warm water
- beaters
- construction paper

Beat flakes and water until they are fluffy and will hold their shape. This can be given to children and molded to make snowmen and other "s" objects. Food coloring can be added to some. Allow to dry before moving. Additional details can be drawn on the paper around the snowman.

String Painting

You will need:
- paper
- tempera paint
- string cut into 1 foot lengths

Begin by dripping paint onto students' papers. Each child makes designs by dragging string through the paint and around the paper.

Sponge Painting

You will need:
- flat sponges
- tempera paint
- paper

Cut sponges into small pieces. (Some may be cut into "s" shapes such as a sun, a star, a square, the letter "s," etc.) Pour paint into a shallow dish. Children dip their sponges into the paint and press them onto the paper to form designs. Both sponge and string painting can be used to make attractive wrapping paper.

Sand Pictures

You will need: fine, white sand
    powdered paint
    glue
    paper

Make various colors of sand by dividing it into several portions and mixing each portion with a different color of dry powdered paint. Students can draw pictures or designs and cover them with glue. They then sprinkle the different colors of sand on the glue while it is still wet. Allow the pictures to dry and then shake off excess sand.

Seed Pictures

You will need: various types of seeds
       (Ask children to bring in seeds from fruit, flowers, or plants.)
    vegetables, dried peas, beans, etc.
    glue
    heavy paper

Children can draw designs or pictures on paper and cover them with glue. The seeds can be put on the glue and allowed to dry.

Sewing Cards

You will need: copies of the patterns on page 223
    paper punch
    heavy paper or thin cardboard
    glue
    strands of yarn (threaded with blunt needles or one end wrapped
       firmly with tape)

Duplicate the patterns on the next page. Glue them on heavy paper or thin cardboard. Trim the edges so that the punch can easily reach the black circles. Punch out all black circles. (Some older children may be able to do this.) Have students connect the holes by "sewing."

Sewing Card Patterns

"S" Games

Simon Says

Give directions to children that begin with the "s" sound, such as skip, sit, stop, stand, squat, stretch your arms, spin, sing, slide, salute, swing your leg, or smile. If the direction is given without starting with the words, "Simon says," the group is not to follow the direction. Very young children should not be made to leave the game if they make a mistake.

String Game

You will need: a ball of string
one small treat for each child

Prepare this activity before the children enter the room. Cut a long piece of string for each child. Tie a small treat to one end of the string. Wind the string all around the room. Give the free end of the string to the child and have him wind it up to find the end with the treat.

Statues

An adult or mature child should be selected as the first twirler. The twirler takes one child at a time by the hand and swings him around in a circle and lets go. The player tries to end up in a funny position that he can hold. When all the children have been twirled, the spinner looks at all the statues and decides which one is the funniest. The statues must not talk, laugh, or move or they will not be selected. The winner is the twirler for the next game.

"S" Science & Math

Sprouting Seeds

You will need: paper towel
clear glass container such as a drinking glass or jar
bean seeds

Cut a paper towel to fit around the inside of the glass container. Add water to make the towel wet. Place the seeds between the paper towel and the glass. Keep the paper towel wet and the seeds will sprout in a few days. Children will be able to see the stem and the root. If you wish the seeds to continue to grow, plant in soil for nourishment. You might sprout other seeds and compare them. You class could even start a small indoor garden.

Take a Look at Spiders

A good book for an introduction is *Are you a Spider?* by Judy Allen and Tudor Humphries (Kingfisher, 2003).

Pass around live spiders (one to a jar) or pictures of spiders so children can look at them while you discuss and ask questions about them. (Can students count how many legs the spider has?) Children who are afraid should not be made to hold the jars.

Spiders have eight legs.	True insects have six.
Spiders have only two body parts.	Insects have three main body parts.
Do you think spiders can fly?	Spiders have no wings.
Do you think they will hurt you?	Some spiders bite, but only a few have poison strong enough to hurt humans.
Look for silk in the jar.	Almost all spiders spin silk.
Can you see eyes or antennae?	They have no antennae, but they often have many eyes.

Before your discussion, check inside and outside for webs. When you take a walk with your class, stand near a web and see if a child can spot it. Ask if they know why spiders build webs. (They build webs to catch their food.)

Take a Look at Snails & Slugs

A good book for an introduction is *Are you a Snail?* by Judy Allen and Tudor Humphries (Kingfisher, 2003).

Pass around garden snails and water snails (which can be purchased at a fish store) in jars or pictures of snails. A few magnifying glasses would be helpful. As these are being passed, discuss snails and ask questions about them.

Can you see how the snail moves?	It has a long flat foot that helps it move. It makes a layer of slime to help it move along.
Can you see what protects its soft body?	The hard shell.
We will want to return these snails to a damp, wet place very soon.	Snails need to keep their bodies wet. If they dry up, they will die.
Count how many feelers (tentacles) you can see.	Many have two short ones and two long ones with the eyes at the end of the long ones.

Look in damp, dark places for slugs. Good places to find them are in gardens and under logs. Explain that a slug is a snail without a shell.

"S" Numerals

Have children count "s" objects (stars, squares, spoons, straws) into piles of sixes and sevens. Give stars and/or stickers to children who can count to and recognize the numerals 16, 17, and the numbers 60 through 79.

"S" Art

Snails

This would be a good activity to do after observing snails (see page 226).

You will need: colored clay

pipe cleaners cut in long and short sections

(roll one end of each long section into a small circle for an eye)

Have each child roll the clay into a long tube. Each tube is then rolled up with the end bent over for the head. Add a flat piece of clay to the bottom for the foot. Poke two long pipe cleaner sections to the top of the head with the circles (eyes) on top. Put one short pipe cleaner on each side of the head.

"Square" Pictures

You will need: paper squares (in many sizes, colors, textures)

glue

sheet of paper for background

Children first arrange, then glue squares on paper to create their own pictures or designs.

"S" Foods

Salad Bar

This activity is good for snack time or lunch if children stay all day.

You will need: salad ingredients

        bowls

        forks, spoons

        dressings (seed dressings such as celery or poppyseed)

Ask each child to bring in one salad ingredient item. Be sure to include the "s" items spinach and scallions. Each child can prepare their own salad and should be encouraged to try at least one new ingredient.

Syrup

You will need: 1 cup light corn syrup

        ½ cup brown sugar

        ½ cup water

        maple flavoring

        1 tblsp. butter or margarine

        cooking pot

        hot plate

        large spoon

        crackers

        knife(for spreading)

Cook and stir the first three ingredients until dissolved. Add a dash of the maple flavoring and the butter or margarine. When cool, have children spread on crackers to taste.

228

Silly Sandwiches

You will need: two slices of bread per child
some simple sandwich fillings
    (cheese, peanut butter, jelly)
small food items cut up for decorations
    (raisins, nuts, seeds, fruits, vegetables)

Children prepare their sandwiches using bread and fillings and decorate the tops with food items. Peanut butter can be used to hold the items in place.

Soup

As an introduction to this activity, read *Stone Soup*, by Ann McGovern (Scholastic, 1986).

You will need: a large pot
hot plate
bowls
spoons
soup recipe
soup ingredients*

An adult should do any cutting required, but children may add ingredients. They can discuss the color, shape, texture and taste of the raw and then cooked ingredients. This could be planned for a lunch if children stay all day. You may also want to include a salad bar.

*Note: You may want to ask parents to donate ingredients.

230

"T" Vocabulary and Oral Expression

Introducing "T"

Introduce "t" words through conversation, illustrations, and questions. (Do you know what a tailor does? What part of a pencil is the tip? Describe how you would trace something.)

Names		**Animals**	**Food**	**Opposites**
Ted	Tom	toad, tadpole	tangerine	take–give
Terry	Tim	turtle	taffy	top–bottom
Toby	Tammy	tiger	tea	tight–loose
Tina	Teresa	toucan	tomato	together–apart
Theo	Tracy	tortoise	tuna	true–false
Trudy	Tad	tarantula	turkey	tender–tough
Taylor	Todd	termite	turnip	
Tyler	Tony	terrier		**Homonyms**
				tail–tale
				tea–tee
				toe–tow
				two–to–too

"T" Objects

Ask, "Can you tell me about any of the following things?" (Make a note of those that no one can describe and provide pictures at a later date.)

tablet	tambourine	tack	toast
taxi	tower	ticket	tag
trail	trophy	trunk	tube
trowel	triangle	tassel	town
telescope	toadstool	tulip	torch
timer	turnstile	tank	track
tent	totem pole	target	trousers

Tongue Twisters

- Ask the children to repeat in unison after you. Then ask if anyone would like to try to say a tongue twister as fast as possible alone.

    Tom took the trowel to transplant tulips.
    Tangerines and tea taste terrific.
    Today, Terry's teacher traced triangles.
    Teddy and Tracy traveled by truck to town.
    Toby Toad tossed Tyler Turtle a tiny tadpole.
    Trudy tried Tuesday to teach Tina tennis.
    Tim Tortoise tricked Teddy Toad two times.

- Now ask students to add one or more "t" words to the following to make tongue twisters:

    Trudy Tiger tried...
    Tommy took ten...
    The twins talked to...
    Tammy had trouble with the...
    Terry traded her two toy trains for Todd's...
    The tubby triplets toddled to...

- Tell the children to answer "yes" or "no" to the following questions and to explain why they answered as they did.

    Can a tablet taste turkey?   *Can a tree play tag?*
    Would you tickle a tiger?   *Can trousers trot?*
    Would you toast a trailer?   *Can a tank talk?*
    Could a tourist be tardy?   *Does a teacher use tacks?*
    Could a toy top tilt?   *Might a tailor wear a tie?*

"T" Art and Activities

Use Your Senses

Sense of Touch

1. Duplicate the letter "T" on page 230.
2. Cover with glue. Stick on small pieces of tissue paper.
3. Have students close their eyes, then feel the page.

Prepare Touching Bags

Give each child a paper bag. Take a walk outside and ask the children to place three or four items in their bags that they find laying on the ground, such as sticks, rocks, or leaves. You might suggest that items be "bigger than your thumb, but smaller than your fist." Then let students exchange bags and see if they can identify what's in the bags by reaching in and feeling. Return the items to the areas where they were found.

Sense of Smell

1. Duplicate the letter "T" as described above.
2. Cover with glue. Sprinkle with thyme, tarragon, or dry tea leaves.
3. Have students close their eyes, then smell the page.

Sense of Taste

Ask the children to close their eyes. Give each a piece of taffy (a common flavor). See if they can identify the flavor by taste alone. Try some tart foods (sour cherries, lemons, grapefruit, limes, etc.). Let students try a taste of a tangerine, a tomato, and a turnip.

Sense of Hearing

Hide a ticking timer in the room. The person who finds it may hide it the next time. Listen to music played by a trumpet, trombone and a tuba, each playing alone.

Sense of Sight

Bring in a telescope for the children to set up outside. Ask them to describe what they can see through it that they cannot see with the naked eye.

Play "I Spy." Items around the room might include towels, a television, a toy train, a top, trucks, and tools.

Toothpick Art

Have a good supply of round, flat and colored toothpicks. Ask the children to draw pictures or designs using straight lines only. Using pointed glue bottles, have them cover the lines on their drawings with glue and lay the toothpicks on the glue. When dry, they can fill in details using crayons and markers. Children might also want to make toothpick "T"s.

Another toothpick art activity students might like is making three-dimensional figures using raisins and toothpicks. Clay or foam can be used for a base. Some "T" objects could be made in this activity.

Toothpaste Art

Squeeze toothpaste into small mounds on paper. Mix in drops of various colors of food coloring. Students can use old toothbrushes, toothpicks and other washable items around the classroom to draw with the toothpaste on paper.

Texture Hunt

Take a walk inside and/or outside. Have students look for and identify things that are sharp, dull, hard, soft, bumpy, smooth, rough, slippery, etc.

Truck Day

Read to your class from *The Truck Book*, by Harry McNaught (Random House, 1978), and *I Want to be a Truck Driver*, by Dan Liebman (Firefly Books, 2001).

Ask each child to bring in a favorite truck to share with the class. (Have extra available for those who forget or have none.) Let each child describe how his truck might be used and what it might carry. Lay out roads on a section of your classroom floor or on the playground. Use paper or chalk. Make tunnels for the trucks to travel under. (Small tunnels can be easily made by cutting a round oatmeal container.) Give the children time to play with the trucks, driving them around on the roads. Some children might like to make traffic lights or road signs.

If you know of a parent whose job includes driving a truck, ask him to speak to your class. Perhaps he would bring the truck to a nearby parking lot for the children to see.

Tricycle Races

You can have outdoor tricycle races at any time of the year (even during the winter) as long as there is an area of the sidewalk or playground that is cleared. The races can be done with 3 or 4 tricycles as the children can race in "heats" and the winners compete until you have one champion. Give everyone a prize for being terrific on tricycles.

Tie-Dye T-Shirts

Ask each child to bring in one white T-shirt. Be sure parents know how the T-shirts will be used ahead of time. Have a few extra on hand for students who forget. Put different colors of diluted food coloring or dye into different containers. Have children fold their T-shirts into squares or rectangles and dip the corners into different containers. Another way to color the shirts is to tightly wrap rubber bands around different parts of the shirt and then dip the shirt in the dye. The dye will not reach the ringed areas of the shirt that have been rubber banded. Unfold the shirt and allow it to dry. (This activity can also be done with napkins, cloth scraps, or sheets. Have children wear smocks when working.)

Triangle Art

Duplicate the triangles on page 238. Make one or more pages for each child. Show them some of the creatures and designs below and/or draw some examples on the blackboard. Ask the children to color, cut out, and paste their own triangle creations on sheets of paper.

Triangle Patterns

238

"T" Movement

Tug of War

Make a soft rope to "tug." Braided strips of cloth work well. Make a line and have each team or player stand an equal distance from the line opposite each other. The object is to try to pull the other team or player over the line by tugging on the rope.

Tumbling

Use mats and teach children some simple tumbling feats such as rolls, leaps, somersaults, etc.

Tag

Teach children the following games of tag.

"T" tag Discuss first the objects around the room that begin with the letter "t" (table, T.V., trucks, trains, etc.). One person is chosen to be the caller and says, "Run." All players move about the room. When the caller says, "Stop," each player must place his hand on an object that begins with the letter "t." The caller tries to tag a player before the player touches an object. If this is done, the tagged player becomes the caller.

Tail Tag Give children large sheets of paper and ask them to draw and cut out a large, long animal tail. You may wish to show pictures of animals with long tails for ideas. Attach one tail to the back of each child's waist with masking tape. The object of the game is for the player chosen to be "it" to tag another player's tail.

Target Toss
Draw a large target and place it on the floor. Have children try to hit the bull's eye on the target by tossing a bean bag. Some will need a demonstration of the difference between throwing and tossing.

Tightrope Walking

Make a line across the floor using a wide strip of tape. Have children walk heel to toe on the line pretending they are tightrope walkers. Children with good balance might like to try walking on tiptoes. A low balance beam could also be used for this activity.

Twist, Twirl, Trot and Tap Dance
Demonstrate how to twist, twirl, trot and tap dance to music. Play tapes or recordings and have children do the "t" movements to the beat. An adult or child acting as leader could call out the "t" movement that everyone should do for part of the dance.

240

Turtle Time

Bring a turtle to class for students to observe.

Make play turtles.

Foam–Turn a foam bowl upside down and glue foam peanuts on the underside for legs and one on the top front for the head.

Salt Clay–(Mix one cup salt, 4 cups flour, 1½ cups cold water.) Form oval clay body. Make smaller balls for head and feet. Moisten them and attach to the body. Dry overnight. Paint with poster paints when dry.

Walnut Shells–Glue paper legs and a head to a large half of a walnut shell. Put a marble under the shell and the turtle will "roll."

Turtles can also be made from paper plates and rocks.

Turtle Candies

Directions for 1 candy: (Multiply the ingredients by the number of candies you wish to make.) Arrange 4 pecan halves, flat sides down with ends meeting in the center, on a wax paper-lined cookie sheet. Flatten one caramel and place in the center of pecan group. Melt six to eight semisweet chocolate chips and pour over caramel, leaving the nut tips showing. Store in a cool place until firm.

"T" Math

Orally review the numerals that begin with the "t" sound. Write them on the board as the children repeat them. (Include 2, 10, 12, and 20 through 29. With more mature children you may wish to go beyond 29.) Then ask for volunteers to go up to the blackboard and follow your directions. Examples: Draw a line *under* the number 10. Draw a line *above* the number 22. Put a dot *on* the number 2.

Typing Time

Bring in one or more old keyboards. Demonstrate how to type just one key at a time. Give each child an opportunity to use the keyboard. (Have an aide or helper sit with the students the first time, if one is available.) Have them practice typing the letter "t," the alphabet, their names, or any other words and letters they wish. Make a list of objects in the room that begin with "t." Print the "t" words on cards, let students copy them on the keyboard, cut them out, and place them on the matching items in the room. (Some "t" objects in your room might be table, tape recorder, toy truck, train, and timer.) Since many children have early exposure to computers, you may wish to duplicate the keyboard on page 243 and use it for discussion and practice.

242

Typing Keyboard

Duplicate this page so each child has a copy. Use it for discussion and practice. Mature children may use it to learn how to place their fingers on the "home keys."

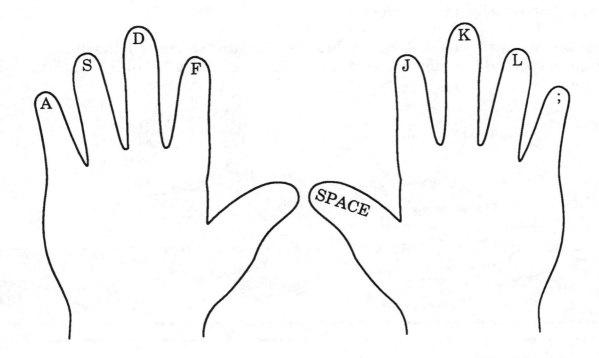

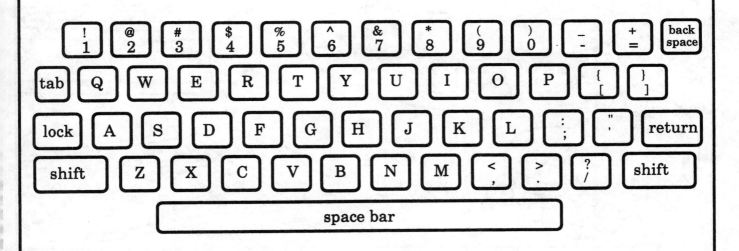

"T" Foods

"T" Toast

Cut bread slices into "T" shapes. Toast the bread. Let children spread their favorite topping (butter, jelly, etc.) on the toast.

Variation: Make "T" sandwiches. Cut bread slices into the shape of the letter "T." Give each child two and ask him to make a sandwich by adding a "T" filling, such as turkey or tuna.

Taco Time

Buy or make tacos. Have fillings that children may use to fill their tacos. Include lettuce, cheese, etc. Be sure to include tomatoes and tomato sauce.

Tasty Tarts

Make or bring in prepared tapioca pudding. Fill tart shells with the pudding. Let children add some "terrific toppings." (Shredded coconut, chocolate, candy sprinkles, and whipped cream would work well.)

"U" Vocabulary and Oral Expression

Introducing "U"

Introduce "u" words through conversation, illustrations, and questions. Have you ever seen the umpire at a baseball game? Do you know what he does? What do you think a ukulele is? What different places have you seen umbrellas? Are they just used for rain? What different people can you think of that wear uniforms? Do you know some things that are underground?

When you put "un" in front of many words, it gives that word the opposite meaning. An example is happy—**un**happy. Have students make each word below opposite in meaning by adding "un" to the beginning of the word.

buckle	button	cork	comfortable
cover	dress	fold	healthy
kind	lucky	pack	tie
true	usual	wind	zip

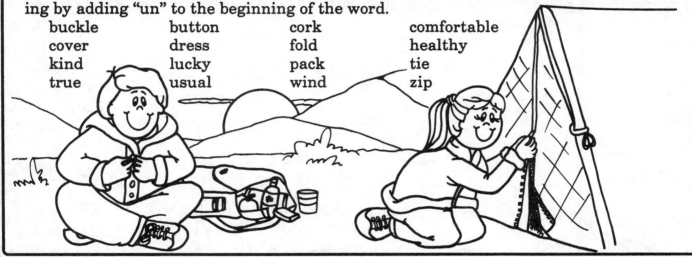

Tongue Twisters

Ask children to repeat in unison after you. Then ask if anyone would like to try to say a tongue twister as fast as possible alone.

Upton was under the umbrella.   *Ursula is unhappy with her uniform.*

Uncle Ulysses usually plays the ukulele.

Tell the children to answer "yes" or "no" to the following questions and explain why they answered as they did.

Can a ukulele be unhappy?   *Can The United States of America carry an umbrella?*

Would unicorns wear underwear?

"U" Activities

Umbrella Day
Read *The Umbrella*, by Jan Brett (Putnam Juvenile, 2004) and *The Thingamabob*, by Il Sung Na (Knopf Books for Young Readers, 2010).

Umbrella Parades
Ask children to bring in their umbrellas. Have extras to take turns if there are fewer umbrellas than students. Go outside and have an umbrella parade (to keep the rain, clouds, and snow away or for shade on a sunny day). Sing while you parade.
Duplicate the pattern on the following page, make the umbrellas, and have an inside parade. Stick small paper parasols in cupcakes and have umbrella cupcakes for a snack.

Umbrella Pattern

Duplicate this page for each child. Tell them to color and decorate the plain sections of the umbrella any way they wish and then to cut the umbrella out along the solid lines (including the one line that goes to the center). A crease should be made along each dotted line. Spread glue on the sections marked "glue" and pull those sections under the two sections on the other side of the cut so that the glue attaches the sections and the paper forms a pointed umbrella. Add a handle by pushing a stick or unsharpened pencil through the center. To make a curved handle, twist two or more large pipe cleaners together, poke one end into the umbrella top and curve the other end.

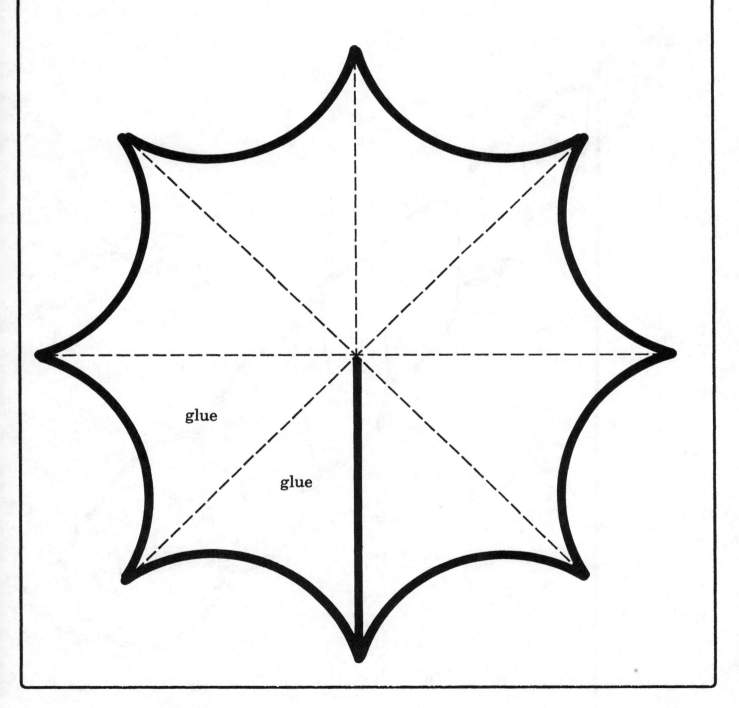

Unicorns
Pin the Horn on the Unicorn
Duplicate the horn pattern below and the unicorn pattern on page 251. You may wish to enlarge the unicorn pattern by using the overhead projector. Blindfold the children and give them each a "horn" that has a tape loop on the back. Play the game the same way "Pin the Tail on the Donkey" is played.

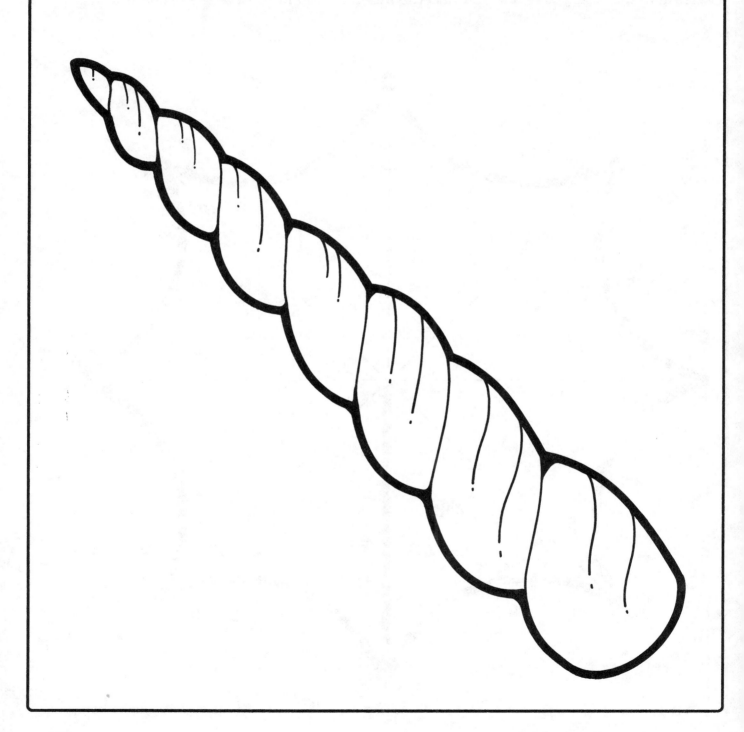

Unicorn Pattern

Make Ugly Duckling Cookies

Read *The Ugly Duckling*, by Hans Christian Andersen. Make or bring in large, round, flat cookies. Have raisins and pointed frosting tubes for decorating. Copy the illustration below onto the blackboard demonstrating to the children how to make ugly faces on their cookies. Then show how they will turn into happy faces by turning the cookies upside down.

Play I Unpacked My Grandmother's Trunk

Have children sit in a circle. Fill a small, light suitcase with items that begin with different letters of the alphabet. The first child removes an item and says, "I unpacked my grandmother's suitcase and took out a ____ that begins with the letter (or sound) ____." The suitcase is then passed to the next child who must repeat what the first child said plus add another item. This goes on until the suitcase is unpacked. Some children might need help when the list begins to grow. The suitcase can be packed again adding new items the children find around the room.

Unbirthday Party

On a day when no child has a birthday, have an "unbirthday party."

Upside Down Cupcakes

Sprinkle a little brown sugar, a half-teaspoon of margarine and some cut-up drained canned fruit in the bottom of each section of a cupcake pan. Prepare a cake mix following directions for cupcakes. Bake and immediately turn upside down. Serve warm. Enjoy with an upside-down sundae.

Upside Down Sundaes

Prepare a selection of ice cream toppings. Have children put a scoop of topping in the bottom of their dish. Put a scoop of ice cream on top of the topping.

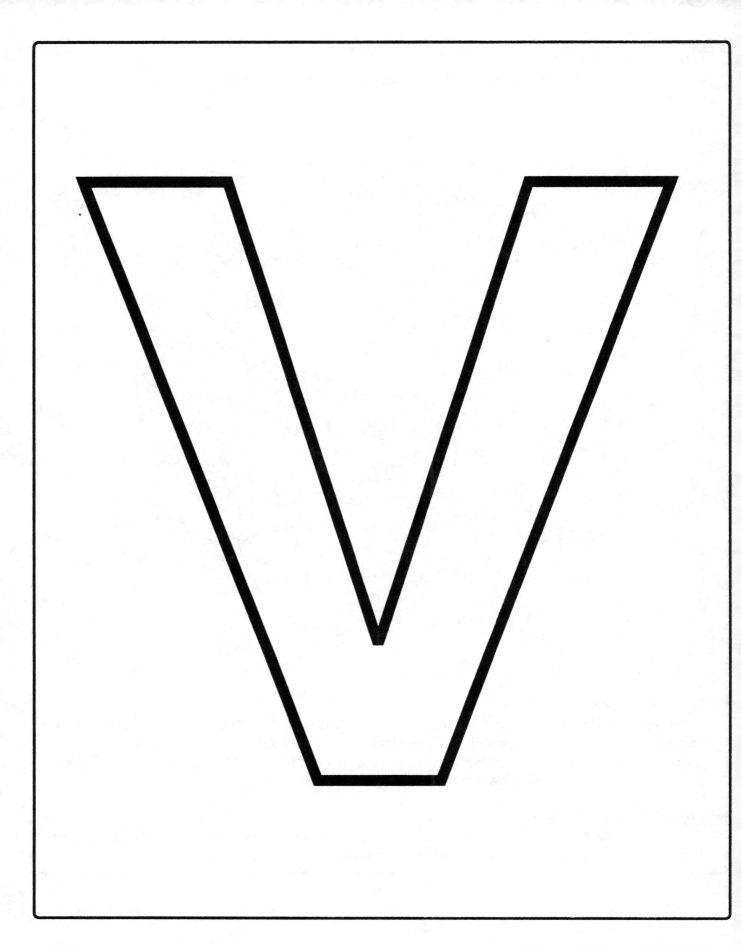

254

255

"V" Vocabulary and Oral Expression

Introducing "V"

Introduce "v" words through conversation, illustrations, and questions. (What did you do on your favorite vacation? If a house is vacant, what does that mean? What is a vegetarian?)

Names

Veronica	Victoria	Vincent	Virgil
Vivian	Victor	Virginia	Vera
Violet	Valerie	Vaughn	Vito
Vanessa	Vernon	Vanna	

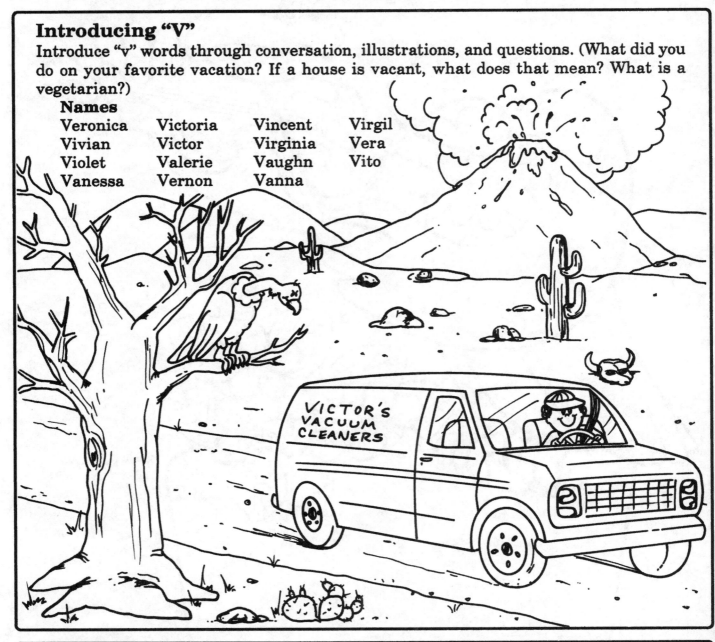

"V" Objects

Ask, "Can you tell me about any of the following things?" (Make a note of those things that no one can describe and provide pictures at a later date.)

vase	visor	village	veterinarian
veil	vacuum	violet	vine
vulture	van	volcano	

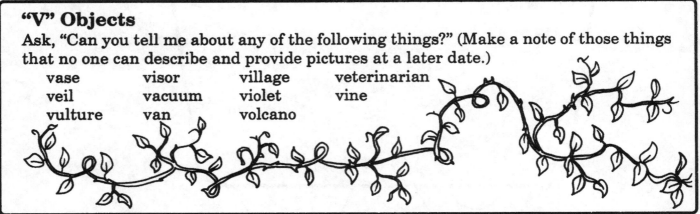

"V" Questions

Tell the children to answer "yes" or "no" to these questions and to explain why they answered as they did.

Can a van vacuum?   Do some visors have vents?

Can you view a video?   Does a veterinarian give vaccinations?

Are some vases valuable?   Do some vegetables grow on vines?

Tongue Twisters

- Ask children to repeat in unison after you. Then ask if anyone would like to try to say a tongue twister as fast as possible alone.

Victor views videos.   *Vera moved into the vacant valley.*

The vase vibrated.   *Valerie wore a valuable, velvet vest.*

Viv vacuumed the van.   *Vic Vulture visited Vernon Vole.*

- Ask the children if they can add one or more "v" words to the following to make tongue twisters:

Virginia has a violet...

The veterinarian came for a...

Vanessa voted for...

Victor gave a velvet valentine to...

Put the violets in a...

Vito has a valuable...

"V" Activities

Use Your Senses

Sense of Touch
1. Duplicate the letter "V" on page 254.
2. Cover with glue. Lay small strips of velvet, velveteen, or velour on the glue.
3. Have students close their eyes and then feel the page.

Sense of Smell
Tell children to close their eyes. Pass around two wads of cotton, one dabbed in vinegar, one in vanilla. See if anyone can distinguish the "v" liquids using his sense of smell.

Sense of Hearing
Listen to a recording of violin and viola music played separately. Play the recordings more than once to see if the children can hear any differences between the two instruments. Record each child reciting a "v" tongue twister. Play the recordings and see how many children can identify the different voices.

Sense of Taste
Have a vegetable tasting party. Be sure to include some of the less common vegetables to give children new tasting experiences.

Sense of Sight
View a "v" video (*The Velveteen Rabbit*, for example). Play "I Spy." Place "v" items around the room, such as a vase, a toy van, vines, vegetables, etc.

Visor Day
Send a note home telling parents that children may bring or wear a visor to school on a specific day. (Some adult visors do not adjust small enough for children to wear.) You might mention that you are studying the letter "v" and would be interested in visors that have "v" words on them. Have a few extra for those who do not have one. Give each child an opportunity to tell something about his visor, such as where it came from, where it has been worn, what it is made of, etc. Follow the directions on page 259 and have each child make his or her own visor.

258

Visor Pattern

Color, decorate, and cut out all the parts of the visor. Staple or tape together strips to make one long strip. Apply glue to one corner of the brim and attach one strip end to the dotted placement guide. Adjust the strip length to fit the individual child's head so that second strip end will align with remaining dotted placement guide when glued.

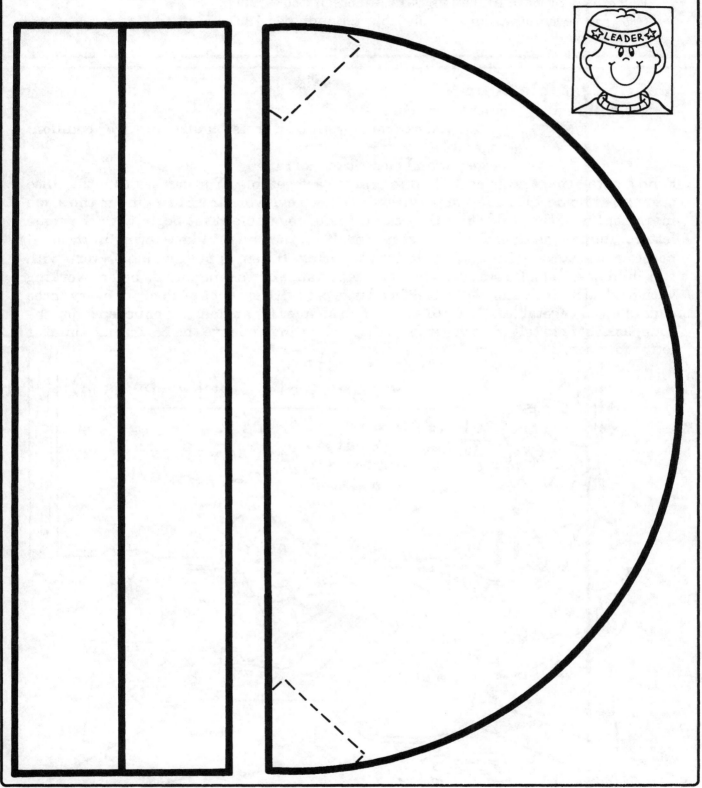

"V" Foods

Have Fun with Vegetables

As an introduction to vegetable activities, read aloud:

The Vegetables We Eat, by Gail Gibbons. Holiday House, 2008.

Vegetables, by Sara Anderson. Sara Anderson Books, 2008.

Growing Vegetable Soup, By Lois Ehlert. Sandpiper, 1991.

Make Vegetable Soup

You will need: chicken or beef stock
(you can make your own or use canned broth or bouillon)
vegetables
large pot and electric or gas range

Send a note home asking each child to bring in a vegetable. (You can ask that they dice them up at home with adult supervision.) To keep everyone from bringing in the same ingredient, ask the children if they can think of vegetables that begin with the same letters (sounds) as their first or last names. If so, they might like to bring in those. If possible, get some extra adult help for the dicing. If help is not available, work with one child at a time. Be sure to stress the importance of washing hands before working with food. Mix stock and vegetables in a large pot, with six cups of stock for every three cups of diced vegetables. Bring to a boil, then simmer for an hour. As children enjoy the soup, ask them to tell what vegetables they are eating and give the beginning sound or letter for each.

Our classy
Vegetable soup - (bring in)

Chris - celery
Tommy - Tomatoes
Carol - carrots
Oscar - onions

Peter - potatoes
Pam - Peas
Gary - garlic

"Veggie" People and Animals

You will need:

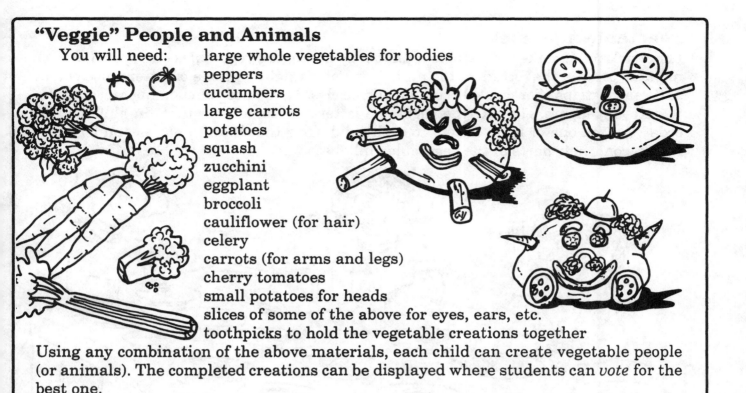

large whole vegetables for bodies
peppers
cucumbers
large carrots
potatoes
squash
zucchini
eggplant
broccoli
cauliflower (for hair)
celery
carrots (for arms and legs)
cherry tomatoes
small potatoes for heads
slices of some of the above for eyes, ears, etc.
toothpicks to hold the vegetable creations together

Using any combination of the above materials, each child can create vegetable people (or animals). The completed creations can be displayed where students can *vote* for the best one.

Vegetable Printing

Put several layers of paper towels in the bottom of a shallow pan. Pour in enough poster paint so the towels are moist with color. Cut vegetables in half. On a large half of a vegetable, cut out a "v" for printing. You can use peppers, the cut end of celery, carrots, cucumbers, radishes, etc. Press the cut side of the vegetable onto the moist towels and then print firmly on paper. (A large stamp pad could also be used.) This makes interesting designs and can also be used for wrapping paper.

Vegetable Alphabet

For snack time, make a vegetable alphabet by arranging vegetables on paper plates or napkins to form the letters of the alphabet. For straight sections of letters, use carrot and celery strips. For curved sections and circles, have slices of cucumbers, radishes, tomatoes, peppers, etc. Lay the vegetable letters out on a large table in alphabetical order. Assign one or more letters to each child. Give the children plates and let them snack from their parts of the vegetable alphabet.

Vegetable "V"s

Cut as many different vegetables as possible into strips. Some vegetables, such as fresh green beans, could be used without cutting. For snack time, give children plates and have them form one or more vegetable "v"s for their snacks.

Vanilla Snacks

Vanilla Sandwich Cookies—Bring in or have children prepare instant vanilla pudding. Have them make cookie sandwiches by spreading the pudding between two vanilla wafers.

Vanilla Milkshakes—Blend together milk, vanilla flavoring and vanilla ice cream in an electric blender. Pour into small paper cups for children to enjoy.

262

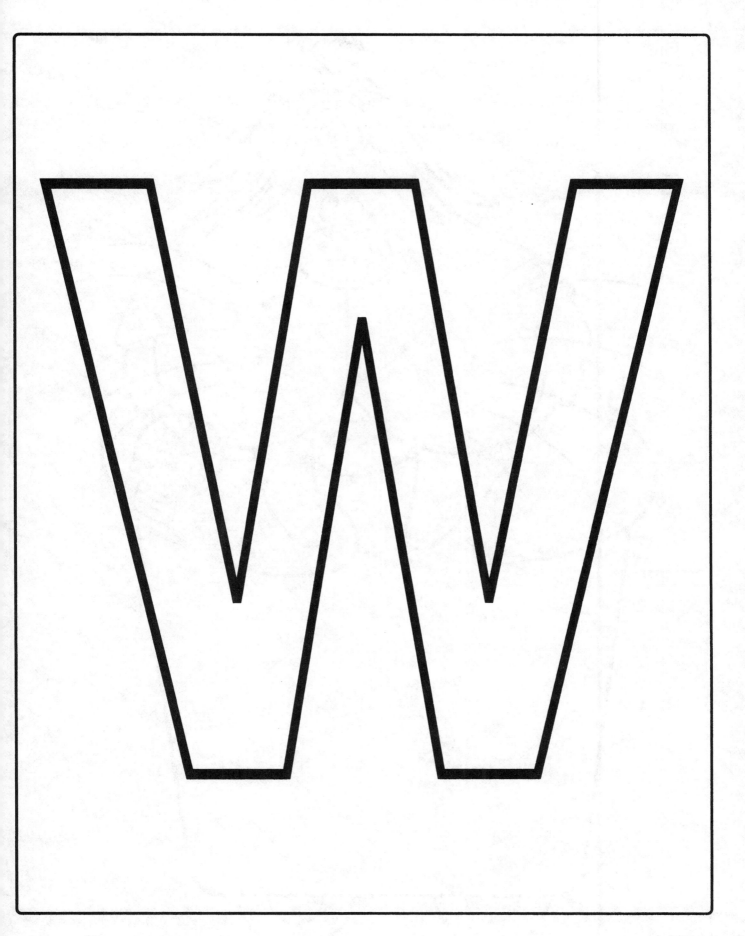

264

"W" Vocabulary and Oral Expression

Introducing "W"

Introduce "w" words through conversation, illustrations, and questions. (What do you know that wiggles? Do you own anything that you have to wind to make go? What does it mean to be wise?)

Names	Opposites	Homonyms	Food	Animals
William	warm–cool	waist–waste	wafers	whale
Wilma	woman–man	wrap–rap	watermelon	woodchuck
Wendy	women–men	wear–where	walnuts	walrus
Wanda	winter–summer	weather–whether	waffles	weasel
Wayne	winner–loser	wait–weight		wolf
Wade	war–peace	way–weigh		worm
Ward	will–won't	wee–we		
Warren	west–east	week–weak		
Wesley	wet–dry	wood–would		
Walter	with–without	won–one		
Winnie	would–wouldn't			

"W" Objects

Ask, "Can you tell me about any of the following things?" (Make a note of those things that no one can describe and provide pictures at a later date.)

waffle	waiter	wallet	wand
watch	web	wagon	wool
wig	wire	walnut	wafer

Tongue Twisters

- Ask children to repeat in unison after you. Then ask if anyone would like to try to say a tongue twister as fast as possible alone.

Wayne went wading Wednesday.   *Wilt's wife watched Willie win.*
Wanda wasp wiggled her wings.   *Wesley Woodchuck walked west.*
Warren's watermelon was wonderful.   *A wild winter wind whistled.*
Walter Walrus washed in warm water.

- Now ask the students if they can add one or more "w" words to the following to make tongue twisters:

Winnie witch woke...
William's watch was...
The winners were...
Wendy Weasel went...
The women will...
Wanda and Wayne's wedding was...

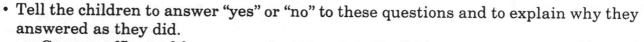

- Tell the children to answer "yes" or "no" to these questions and to explain why they answered as they did.

Can a waffle wash?   *Could a woman worry?*
Does a waitress walk?   *Can you wave a wand?*
Can a wallet weep?   *Can wind wink?*
Could you wear wool clothes?   *Can you wash a wagon?*
Can we have wet weather?   *Can you wind wire?*
Are most wolves wild?   *Does a walrus like water?*
Could a watermelon wave?   *Does a whale have wings?*

"W" Art and Activities

Use Your Senses

Sense of Touch
1. Cut one or more "w"s from thin, flat sponges.
2. Soak the sponges in water and lay them in a flat dish.
3. Ask children to feel the shape of the wet "w."

Sense of Taste
Let students taste walnuts and various flavors of wafers.

Sense of Hearing
- Ask children to sit with their backs to you. Whisper "w" words to them. Have them raise their hands if they think they can repeat the word(s) back to you.
- Give an opportunity for pairs of children to use walkie-talkies.

Sense of Sight
Play "I Spy." When children are out of the room, place items beginning with the letter "w" around the room in clear view. Items might include a watch, the window, water, and pictures of a whale, wolf, worm and witch. Begin a game by saying, "I spy a 'w' object in the room…" and then give a clue as to its identity. The student who guesses correctly may then lead the game. An adult may need to whisper a suggestion for an object or a clue.

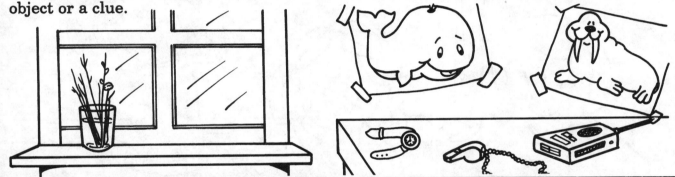

Weaving
Precut heavy paper as shown. Precut paper strips the same length as the heavy paper. Show children how to weave the paper in and out and to glue the ends down.

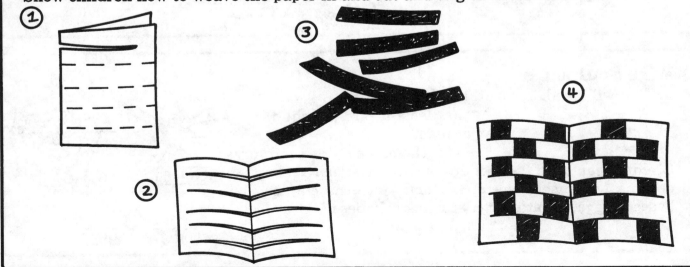

Working with Words

Read aloud the *Best Little Word Book Ever* by Richard Scarry (Golden Book, 2001). Make large word cards for familiar objects around the room. Be sure to include "w" words, such as window, wall, wastebasket, etc. Discuss each word and have the children place the matching card on the object they name. Leave the cards for a few days. Then one morning collect them before the class comes in and see if anyone can place a word in front of the correct object.

Wax Paper Painting

Prepare a sheet for each child in the following manner. Put wax paper on another sheet of paper with the wax side down. Both papers should be the same size and the activity will work best if the sheets are clipped together. The child draws a picture or design on the wax paper, pressing hard so the wax goes onto the paper under it. When finished with the drawing, the child can remove the wax paper and paint over the plain paper. The wax lines will resist the paint and the drawing will appear.

Wire Sculpture

You will need: soft, flexible wire
　　　　　　　　　　(at least a yard per child)
　　　　　　　　clay or foam
　　　　　　　　　　(for the bases of the sculptures)
Children can bend the sections of wire into desired shapes or designs and insert one of the ends into the clay or foam bases. Suggest that they try to make shapes of "w" objects.

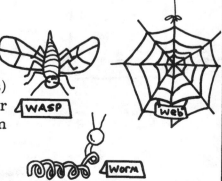

White Day

Ask children to wear and/or bring things to class that are white.

- Let children draw white pictures using chalk, paints or crayons. The drawings may work best if they are done on colored construction paper.
- Have each student make a bleach picture. Cover the work area and children's clothing before letting them begin. Put bleach in saucers that will not tip (or in low dishes). Have children dip cotton swabs into bleach and draw on dark paper.
- Take a "white walk" both inside and outside the building. Keep track of the number of things you and your class see that are white.

clouds
sidewalk
stones
flowers

chalk
paper
glue
lights

Let's Talk About Worms

Go outside and have a worm "hunt." Prepare a box with soil so that one end is damp and the other is dry. (Note the area that the worms prefer.) Discuss with the children where they think they should look for worms.

After collecting worms, discuss the habitats where they were found. Place one on a wet towel and watch how it moves. Turn it upside down and watch how it rights itself. Put it on a clear glass plate and hold it up to light. Let students look at the worm through the bottom. They may see the intestinal tract, beating heart, and blood vessels. Have them measure and compare the length of the worms.

*Note: Earthworms absorb oxygen through their damp skin so it is important to keep them moist. If their skin dries out, they will suffocate.

270

Have An Earthworm Race

Select hard, bare ground that is shady. Scratch out a circle that is one to two feet in diameter. Put the worms in the center of the circle. The first one to crawl out of the circle is the winner. When the race is over, be sure to return the worms to the damp, loose soil.

Discuss how worms are used by fishermen, why you see them on the sidewalks after a rain, why farmers and gardeners like worms, and what they eat and who likes to eat them.

After students have discussed and seen real worms, let them make worms out of clay or play dough.

Movement

Read aloud *Wiggle Giggle Tickle Train*, by Nora Hilb and Sharon Jennings (Annick Press, 2009). Encourage children to act out the activities shown in the book.
Before heading outside for a class walk, read *I Went Walking*, by Sue Williams (HMH Books, 1996). When you return to the class, ask children to share what they saw.
Have a backwards-walking race.

"W" Food

Witches' Brew

Children may enjoy making up their own recipe for witches' brew, or you can use the recipe below.

Witches' Brew
You will need:
14 oz. powdered orange drink mix
⅔ cup instant tea (decaffeinated)
2 envelopes lemonade mix
2 cups sugar
2 teaspoons cinnamon
2 teaspoons powdered cloves

Mix the above ingredients. Add 1 to 2 teaspoons to one cup of boiling water. Direct children to carefully stir until cool enough to drink.

Watermelon Ice Cream

Cut a watermelon in half. Scoop out the insides leaving only a green edge. (Save the scooped out watermelon for a "w" snack.) Fill the empty watermelon shells with pink ice cream or sherbet to which you have added chocolate chips (to look like seeds). Cover and freeze. Then slice a piece for each child.

274

"X" Vocabulary and Activities

Introducing "X"

Very few words in a child's world begin with the letter "x." You may want to ask questions and show pictures if necessary of x-rays and a xylophone. (What are x-rays and why do people have them taken? Did you ever have a toy xylophone?)

Rhyming Words That End With the Letter "x"

box	six	Max	Alex
fox	mix	tax	Rex
ox	fix	wax	flex
		ax	

Show students "ex" words that make the "x" sound.

exit	excited	exercise	explode
exchange	explain	expert	expression

Tongue Twisters

Ask children to repeat in unison after you. Then ask if anyone would like to try to say a tongue twister as fast as possible alone.

Six foxes box.
Max puts wax on his ax.
Rex explains the exercise.

"X" Activities

Play "X" Marks the Spot

Put up a large outline of a human body. Let the children fill in the details, clothes, facial features, etc. Blindfold each child, one at a time, and give him a big letter "X." Play like Pin the Tail on the Donkey, only give each child a different direction, such as, "Put your 'X' on the body on a spot where a person might have a pocket. (...would wear a shoe. ...use a comb, etc.)" There are no winners or losers, just humorous results and lots of laughs.

Use Your Senses

Sense of Touch and Smell

1. Duplicate the letter "X" on page 273.
2. Cover with wax.
3. Have students close their eyes and then feel the page.

Sense of Hearing

Give children the opportunity to listen to and play a xylophone. (You may wish to explain that this word starts with the letter X, but does not contain the "eks" sound.) Ask why they think the bars on the xylophone make different sounds. Then have the children close their eyes while you play a series of notes. Ask them to raise their hands if they hear the notes go higher and touch the floor if they hear the notes go lower.

Sense of Sight

Bring in some x-ray pictures. Ask children how they are different from other photographs and why they might be helpful to doctors and dentists. Children who have had x-rays enjoy sharing their experiences.

X-tra Special X Cookies

Prepare your favorite cookie recipe or roll out plain refrigerator cookie dough. You may make cookies ahead of time or bake them in class. Make the cookies into "x" shapes. Let children make them "x-tra special" by frosting and adding their favorite decorations, such as candies, sprinkles, nuts, etc.

Using X

Make a simple map of your classroom showing tables, desk, etc. Duplicate a copy for each child. Ask them to make an "X" on various places you mention. Some examples could be "Where you are sitting right now," "Where the piano is," etc.

Draw a clock on the blackboard with Roman Numerals with the ten missing. You can also give individual copies to each child. Explain that they will sometimes see Roman Numerals on clocks and that X means 10. Ask them to fill in the missing X on their clocks.

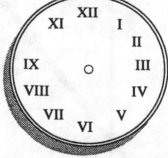

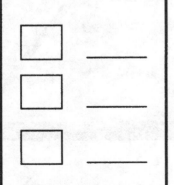

Show how an X is used on a ballot. Make and duplicate a ballot similar to the one shown here. Ask the children to color the top square blue, the middle one red, and the bottom one yellow. Then have them make an X beside the color they like best. Let them help count the ballots after you have collected them.

Cross-Stitch X

Duplicate the pattern below and the patterns on pages 279 and 280. Paste them on the bottom of foam meat trays or thin cardboard and punch holes where indicated. Thread blunt needles with yarn or harden the tips of the yarn with glue. Demonstrate to the class how to make cross-stitches. If additional adult help is not available, work with one or two children at a time to complete the cross-stitching. An alternative to the cross-stitching is to punch holes and let the students do a lacing activity. You may either harden the yarn tips with glue or wrap tape around the end of the yarn to make it easier to lace.

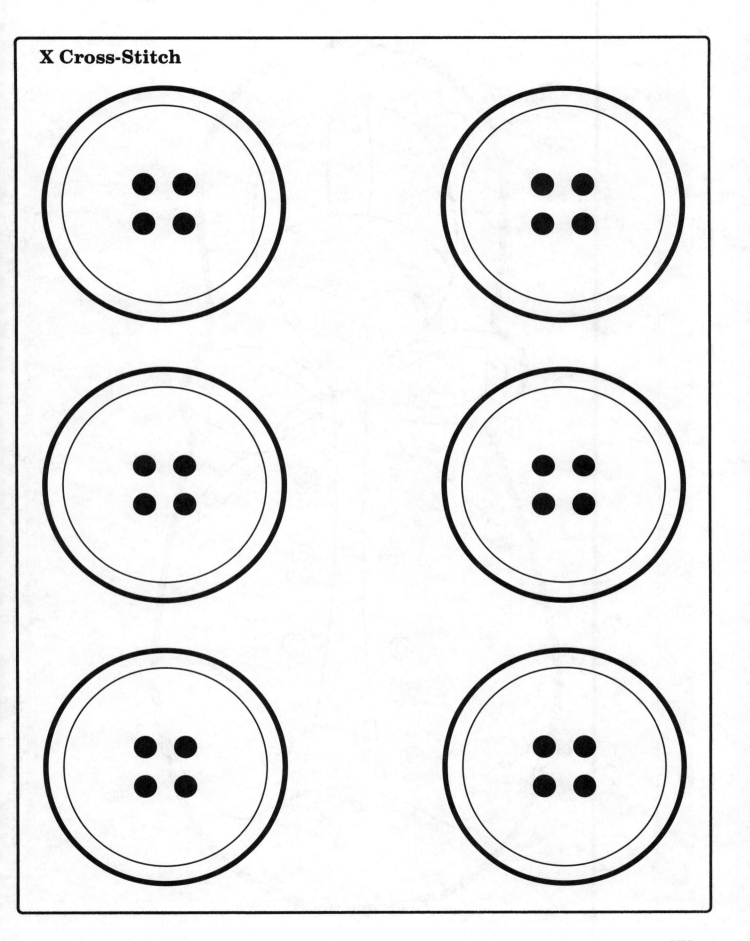

X Cross-Stitch

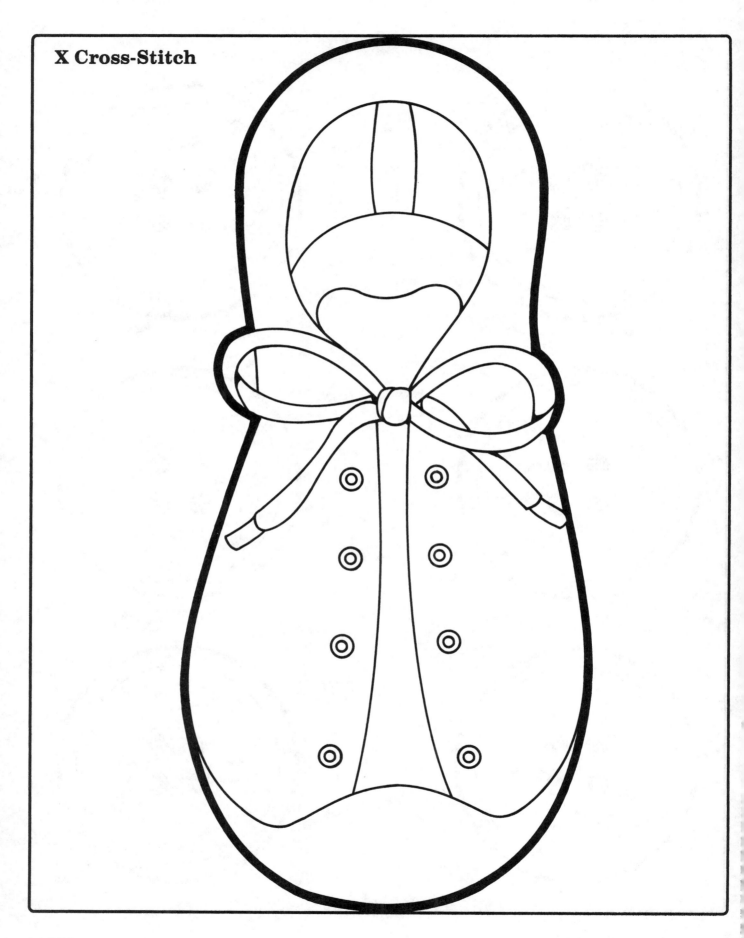

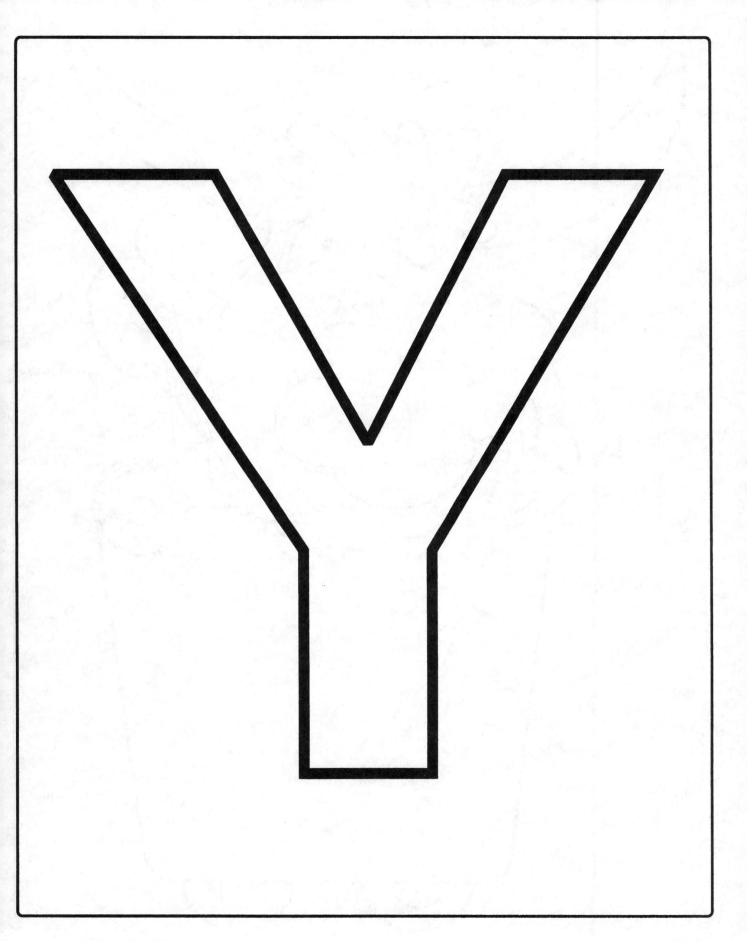

282

"Y" Vocabulary and Oral Expression

Introducing "Y"
Introduce "y" words through conversation, illustrations, and questions. (When you see someone yawn, what do you think? There are two meanings for the word *yard*. Do you know one of them? What color is an egg yolk?)

"Y" Sounds
Who or what might make the following sounds?

yap	yip	yelp
yipee	yoo-hoo	

"Y" Objects
Ask, "Can anyone tell me about any of the following things?" (Make a note of those that no one can describe and provide pictures at a later date.)

yarn	yogurt	yard
yak	yo-yo	yardstick
yam	yacht	

Tongue Twisters
- Ask children to repeat in unison after you. Then ask if anyone would like to try to say a tongue twister as fast as possible alone.

    Yesterday Yancy ate yogurt. *Yvonne yelled, "Yipes! Yellowjackets!"*
    The yearling yelped at the yak. *Every year Yates yodels, "Yellow Bird."*
    Yvonne yanked the yo-yo away
    from the youngster.

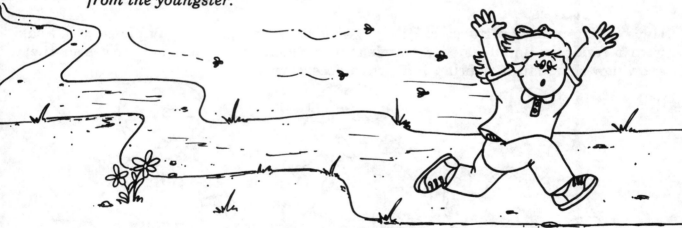

- Tell the children to answer "yes" or "no" to these questions and to explain why they answered as they did.

    Can yarn yawn? *Can a yacht yodel?*
    Could yogurt be yellow? *Could a yachtsman yield?*
    Can a youngster yell?

"Y" Art and Activities

Yarn Art
You will need: white glue mixed with water or liquid starch
strands of different colors of yarn
wax paper

Dip the yarn into the glue or starch. Arrange the yarn on wax paper to form a design or picture. There should be a great deal of overlapping of the yarn. You may wish to demonstrate this. Allow to dry. The yarn should be very stiff. Remove from the wax paper and hang or mount on colored paper to display.

Variation: Arrange yarn strands on the sticky side of contact paper to form designs and pictures. Hang up where the light can shine through.

Yarn Weaving
Students can weave yarn strands in and out of mesh material (the kind used to pack oranges or onions). Different colors can be used to make pictures or designs.

Yarn Pictures
Have children draw pictures or designs with straight lines and simple curves. Soak yarn strands in liquid glue or starch and lay along the lines and curves in their drawings. Cut to fit or overlap yarn when necessary.

Variation: After completing their drawings, children use a pointed white glue bottle and cover their lines with glue. Then lay the yarn strands on the glue.

Yarn Patterns

Duplicate this page so every child has a copy. Have students use either of the methods described at the bottom of page 284 to outline the shapes below with yarn.

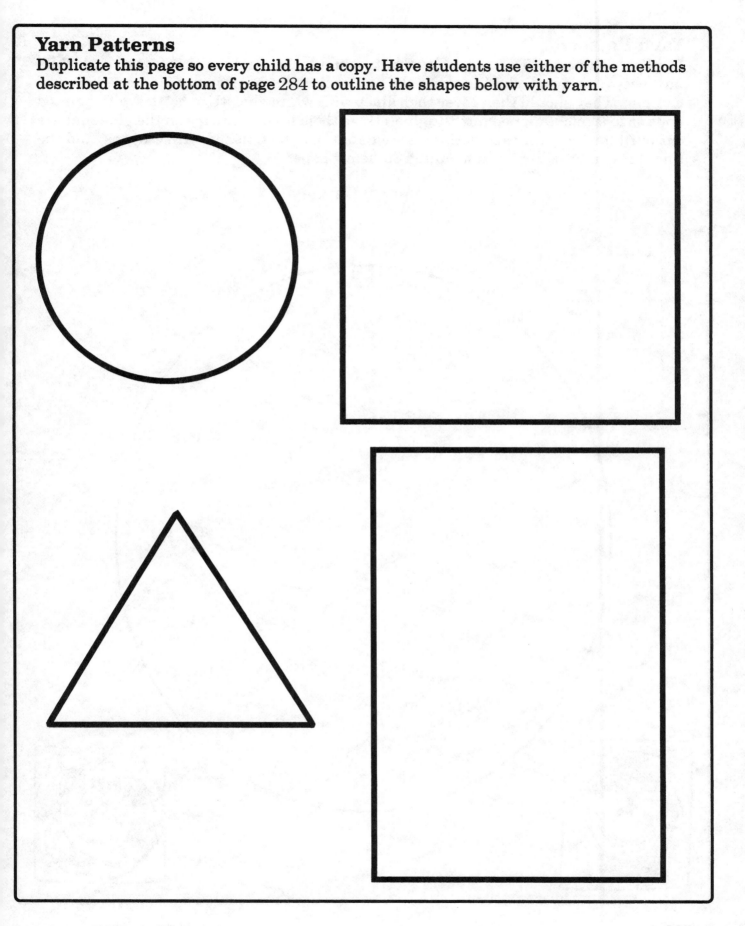

Yarn Pattern

Duplicate this page (or trace the oval onto a blank page and duplicate it) so each child has a copy. Ask each child to make the oval into a face by drawing features, hair and clothing. They should then cover their lines with white glue. (Use bottles with pointed ends or toothpicks dipped into the glue.) Have them lay yarn strips on the glue that are cut to fit (or the yarn can overlap). Face details can be finished with crayons, and the final art can be cut out and mounted on heavy paper.

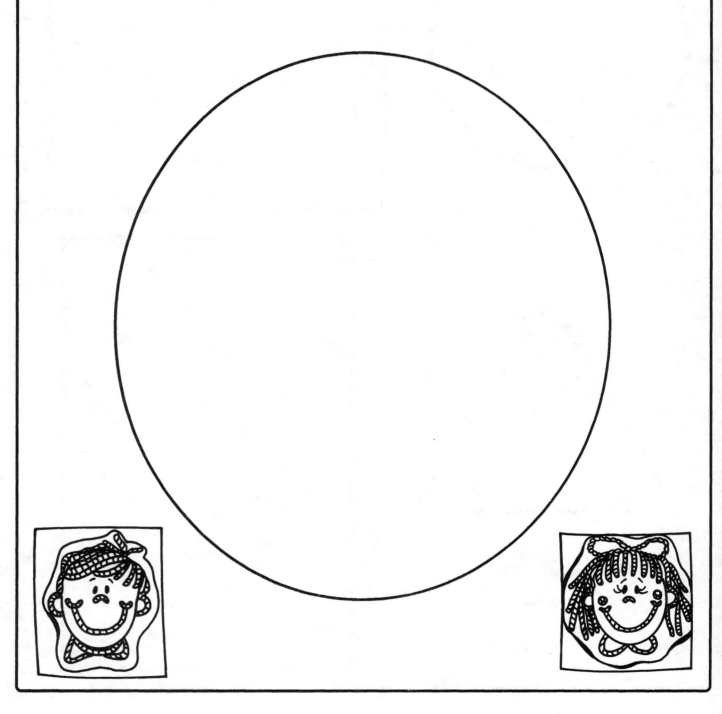

Yellow Day

Ask children to wear and/or bring in something that is yellow.

Read *In My New Yellow Shirt*, by Eileen Spinelli (Henry Holt and Company, 2001) and *Little Blue and Little Yellow*, by Leo Lionni (HarperCollins, 1995).

For snack time, serve yellow cupcakes, bananas, pineapple, and lemonade.

Use Your Senses

Sense of Touch

1. Duplicate the letter "Y" on page 281.
2. Cover it with glue. Lay short strips of yellow yarn on top of the glue.
3. Have students close their eyes and then feel the page.

Sense of Hearing

- Have the class listen to a recording of yodeling. *The Sound of Music* album includes one called "The Lonely Goatherd." Play more than once and ask children to try to yodel at the appropriate time.
- Ask children to try to imitate animals that might yelp, yip or yap.

Sense of Taste

Let students try some bite-size samples of yellow fruits and vegetables such as corn, cheese, yellow apples and tomatoes, bananas, pineapple, wax beans, or summer squash.

Sense of Sight

Play "I Spy." If necessary, put yellow objects around the room, such as yellow toys and school supplies. First play "I spy something yellow." Then you can tell children, "I spy something that begins like 'yes.' " (Yarn, yo-yo, and yardstick are some words to use.)

"Y" Food

Painted Egg Yolk Cookies

Roll out refrigerator cookie dough (available in rolls at grocery stores). Cut into simple shapes, such as circles, squares, etc. Using a knife, cut some dough into the shape of a "Y." Bake according to the directions on the package. When cool, paint with egg yolk paint.

Egg Yolk Paint—For each color, add ¼ teaspoon of water to one egg yolk. Stir in drops of food coloring until the desired color is achieved. Paint the cookies with a watercolor brush. Return cookies to warm oven until egg has solidified.

Yogurt Pops

Mix plain yogurt with frozen juice concentrate to taste. You might like to use a variety of juice flavors to give children a choice. Freeze in small paper cups. Insert ice cream sticks when mixture is partially frozen. When completely frozen, peel off paper cups and enjoy.

Yummy Yams

Many young children have never tasted yams, so this may be a new taste experience for them. Drain one or more cans of yams and let the children mash them. For each can of yams, add a can of crushed pineapple and the juice. Stir together. Cover with marshmallows. Bake for 20 minutes at 350°. Cool and taste. Use a toaster oven if no other cooking facilities are available.

"Z" Vocabulary and Oral Expression

Introducing "Z"
Introduce "z" words through conversation, illustrations, and questions. (Who can come up to the blackboard and draw a zig-zag line? Can someone draw a zero? Did you know that your family has a ZIP code? Does anyone know what a ZIP code is?)

"Z" Objects
Ask, "Can anyone tell me about any of the following things?" (Make a note of those things that no one can describe and provide pictures at a later date.)

zucchini	zipper	zinnia
zoo	zebra	zither

Tongue Twisters
Ask children to repeat in unison after you. Then ask if anyone would like to try to say a tongue twister as fast as possible alone.

Zebra fish zoom. *Zelda zebra walks zig-zag through the zoo.*
Zachary eats zucchini. *Zoologists study zebus and zebras.*
Zelda plays the zither. *Ezra's ZIP code has two zeros.*
Zee zips Zach's zipper. *The camera zoomed in on the zinnias.*

"Z" Art and Activities

Zig-Zag Activities

Movement
Draw or tape zig-zag lines on the floor or playground surface. Ask children to do various movements (walking, heel to toe, running, trotting, skipping, etc.) while remaining on the lines.

Art
Have children practice making zig-zag lines. Then ask them to draw some zig-zag pictures or designs.

Cutting
Duplicate the awards below. Ask children to color, cut out along the zig-zag lines and add phrases (or even "Z" words) to them. Let the children wear their awards.

"Z"s, "O"s, and Zeros

Have each child make a long thin rope of play dough. Break off one section and demonstrate how to form it into the letter "z." Break off another section and form an "O." Explain that when this shape is a numeral, it is called a zero. Have each child form his own "Z" and "O." More mature students would enjoy making the word "zero" using the two shapes they have already made. Demonstrate how to make a play dough "e" and "r" and place between the other two letters.

Cookies

Roll out refrigerator cookie dough and form into "Z"s and "0"s (zeros). Bake and have children frost, decorate and enjoy at snack time.

Variations: Make "e" and "r" cookies also. Have children pick the four cookies needed and place them in correct order to spell the word "zero." Use a cookie cutter or cut around a cardboard pattern to make zebra cookies. Let children make them striped by frosting with pointed tubes.

Zucchini People

Let children create people by using zucchini for bodies. Using toothpicks, body features and parts can be added by attaching cherry tomatoes, cloves, raisins, string beans, etc. Yarn and material scraps can be glued to the figures. Marking pens can add details.

"Z" Alphabet Play

Alphabet Zoo

The speaking parts in this play can be taught by rote to non-reading children. Patterns for stick puppets to use when performing this play are on pages 299 through 305.

Characters:

Ali Gator, Barry Bear, Katie Cow, Donnie Duck, Elmer Elephant, Freddie Fox, Gina Giraffe, Henry Hippo, Iris Ibis, Jerry Jackal, Kari Kangaroo, Lonnie Lion, Millie Monkey, Norman Newt, Ollie Otter, Penny Penguin, Quincy Quail, Roger Rhinoceros, Susie Seal, Tim Tiger, Eunice Unicorn, Vicky Vulture, Wally Walrus, Oxie Ox, Yancy Yak, and Zelda Zebra.

(All the animals are grouped together, looking at Elmer Elephant.)

Elmer Elephant: Gather round. I have news that I know will please you. I have been asked to help plan an alphabet zoo.

All the Animals: Tell us, please tell us what we can do,

To help with your plans for the alphabet zoo.

Elmer: I will call out each letter and we'll all look around,

To see which of us begins with that sound.

I'll begin right away,

With the first letter "A."

Ali Gator: There's no question at all, that I am the one,

To swim in a new zoo should be lots of fun.

Elmer: Letter "B"

Barry Bear: I'll be there, I'll be there, just tell me when,

Please remember to tell them I need a den.

Alphabet Zoo (continued)

Elmer:	Letter "C"
Katie Cow:	If you are planning a farm, then I should do,
	I'll let children pet me and give a soft, "Moo."
Elmer:	Letter "D"
Donnie Duck:	Here I am, the best choice you can make.
	Just remind them I'd like a pool or a lake.
Elmer:	No need to look around for someone for "E."
	It should be me. Don't you agree?
All Animals:	Yes, and a good choice it is, too.
	After all, you're in charge of the alphabet zoo.
Elmer:	Letter "F"
Freddie Fox:	I will be a good addition to any zoo.
	I am smart and will help solve problems for you.
Elmer:	Letter "G"
Gina Giraffe:	I'll wiggle my head since I don't make much sound.
	I think I am the best "G" animal around.
Elmer:	Letter "H"
Henry Hippo:	No doubt about it, I'm sure you all know,
	No zoo is complete without a hippo.
Elmer:	Letter "I"
Iris Ibis:	I will come, but I want a place to wade,
	And a good hiding place where a nest can be made.
Elmer:	Letter "J"
Jerry Jackal:	I'm here and I'll come, but
	I'd like a fenced yard, if one can be found.
	A cage is too small for moving around.

Alphabet Zoo (continued)

Elmer:	Letter "K"
Kari Kangaroo:	When it comes to "K" animals to be in a zoo,
	What could be better than a big kangaroo?
Elmer:	Letter "L"
Lonnie Lion:	As King of the Beasts, I must be in the zoo.
	I'll ask the lioness and cubs to come along too.
Elmer:	Letter "M"
Millie Monkey:	Here I am. I am sure you agree,
	A zoo's not a zoo without a monkey.
Elmer:	Letter "N"

(All animals look around. No one speaks.)

Elmer:	Oh me, oh my, what will we do?
	We have no "N" animal for our alphabet zoo.
Freddie Fox:	I told you I'm smart and quite clever too.
	I'll hunt down an "N" animal and bring him to you.
Elmer:	Oh, thank you. We'll go on and hope "N" is all we lack.
	By the time we reach "Z," fox may be back.
	Letter "O"
Ollie Otter:	I will come and could live with the seal if you wish.
	We both like the water and feed on fresh fish.
Elmer:	Letter "P"
Penny Penguin:	I might be available, if my home is kept cool,
	And it is close to a very cold pool.
Elmer:	Letter "Q"
Quincy Quail:	There aren't many animals that start with a "Q,"
	So you had better take me for your alphabet zoo.

Alphabet Zoo (continued)

Elmer:	Letter "R"
Roger Rhinoceros:	I will polish my horns and scrub myself clean.
	I wish I could smile, so I wouldn't look mean.
Elmer:	Letter "S"
Susie Seal:	I'm right here and willing, but do you suppose,
	I must practice walking with a ball on my nose?
Elmer:	Letter "T"
Tim Tiger:	There are other "T" animals, I know that is true,
	But a zoo's not a zoo without a tiger or two.
Elmer:	Letter "U"
Eunice Unicorn:	I'm a fanciful animal, but you'll need me, it's true.
	There are very few animals that begin with a "U."
Elmer:	Letter "V"
Vicky Vulture:	We vultures are not popular, but I'll have to do.
	There are not many "V" animals for your alphabet zoo.
Elmer:	Letter "W"
Wally Walrus:	I will be glad to join the zoo if you wish,
	But I have a request—daily meals of fresh fish.
Elmer:	Letter "X"
Oxie Ox:	There is no "X" animal that would live in a zoo,
	But "X" is my last sound, so I hope I will do.
Elmer:	Letter "Y"
Yancy Yak:	I will live with the ox as I am that type too.
	A yak "fills the bill" for a "Y" at the zoo.
Elmer:	Letter "Z"
Zelda Zebra:	When you think of a "Z" for your zoo,
	Who else but a zebra would do?

Alphabet Zoo (continued)

(Fox returns carrying a box.)

Freddie Fox: I have found your "N" animal. You will like him. He's cute.

He's a type of a salamander who is called a newt.

Norman Newt: My name is Norman. Your zoo sounds quite neat.

I'll be happy to make your new zoo complete.

All the Animals: Hoorah for the fox, he saved the show,

Our alphabet zoo is ready to go!

"Z" Puppet Patterns

Color and cut out the patterns on the dark line. Tape an ice cream stick, ruler or unsharpened pencil to the back of the pattern to make it into a stick puppet.

Zoo Puppet Patterns (continued)

Zoo Puppet Patterns (continued)

Zoo Puppet Patterns (continued)

Zoo Puppet Patterns (continued)

Zoo Puppet Patterns (continued)

Zoo Puppet Patterns (continued)

Oral Expression Review

Guess My Name

If children are familiar with the first and last names of their classmates, put the initials of one student on the board. See if someone can figure out the name by the sounds of the letters. If no one can answer correctly, give another sound clue. "This person is wearing a shirt with a color that begins with the letter ___ (print the letter *r* on the board without saying it). Variation: Print the first letter of a student's first name only. Play as above.

Add a Word

Have children sit in a circle. One student is selected to begin and says the name of any letter and a word that begins with that letter. The next person must repeat the letter name, say the word, and add another word beginning with the same sound. The game continues until someone cannot repeat all the words or add a new word. Another letter can be started.

306

Review Activities (Movement)

Form a Letter

Prepare the floor by covering as large an area as possible with mats and blankets. Give each child or group a slip of paper on which you have written a letter they are to form with their bodies. The other children should try to recognize the letter. Letters that can be done by one child are *l*, *c*, *r*, and *x*. Two children could do the letters *L*, *T*, *V*, and *H*. Three children might want to try the letters *Z*, *F*, *K*, *N*, or *Y*.

Alphabet Parade

Recite the alphabet in unison and have children line up one behind the other in alphabetical order according to the first letter of their first names. March around the room while playing or singing an alphabet song. Variations: 1.) Line up in alphabetical order according to the first letter of their last names. 2.) Duplicate the capital letters of the alphabet. Make a circle headband for each child and attach a letter to the front. Place one on each child's head. Have them line up in alphabetical order according to their hat letter. If you do not have enough students, paste all the remaining letters on the last hat. Each headband could be decorated before the parade with illustrations of items that begin with the letter.

Alphabet Riddles

Put the letters that are the answers to these riddles on the blackboard so children can be looking at them when you ask the riddles.

Examples: Which letter is a busy little insect? (B)
             What letter is something to drink? (T)
             Which letter is part of your head? (I)
             Which letter is a large body of water? (C)
             Which letter asks a question? (Y)

Action Alphabet Antics

The activity begins with a demonstration by the leader, who says, "I am going to do something that begins with the sound of *S*." The leader can then pantomime *sweeping*, *sleeping* or any other "s" activity. Children guess and the first one who is correct becomes the leader, selects a letter and pantomimes an activity.

Rope Letters

Have children roll out clay into long ropes, break them apart and form them into the letters of the alphabet, the letters in their names or other common words. Many might like to copy simple words that have been printed on the blackboard (such as dog, cat, man, house, etc.).

308

Alphabet Food Review

Eating the Alphabet

Read *Eating the Alphabet*, by Lois Ehlert (Harcourt, Brace, Jovanovich, 1989).
Empty a box of alphabet cereal on a table and have an alphabet "hunt." Ask children to identify letters and/or look for specific letters (such as their initials, familiar words, etc.). Let them use a pointed glue bottle to glue their letter "finds" onto a sheet of paper. Some might like to draw pictures of the sound(s) or the word(s) above the letters. Have an additional box of cereal that can be enjoyed as a snack.

Serve alphabet pasta or soup for a snack. Children will enjoy naming the letters as they eat them.

Alphabet Cookies

Be sure children wash their hands before this and all other cooking activities. Give each one a clean mat or plate dusted with flour and a small ball cut from a roll of plain refrigerator cookie dough. Direct them to dust their hands with the flour (demonstrate how) and roll the dough into a long snake. Assign a letter to each child, give a pattern if necessary, and ask him to form his snake into that letter. You may wish to do one letter as a demonstration. Add candy sprinkles before baking. Bake according to directions on the package. Do a few at a time in a toaster oven if no other cooking facilities are available.

Review-Letter Patterns

Use the letters on the following pages for cookie patterns, letter and sound reviews, word building, etc.

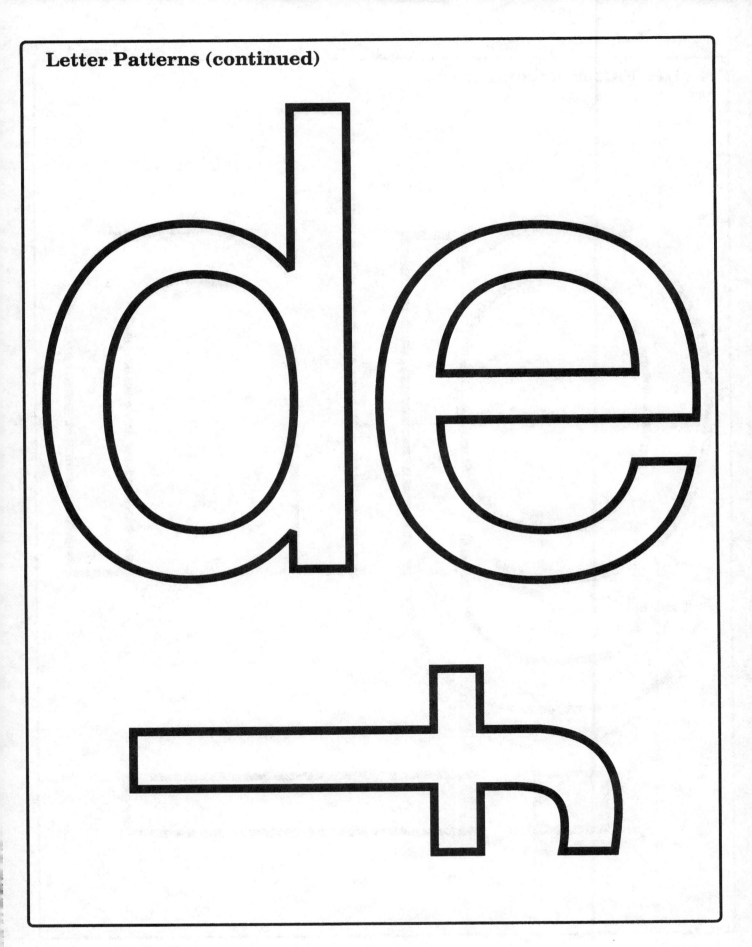

Letter Patterns (continued)

alternate "a" pattern

Letter Patterns (continued)

The letters provided for duplication may differ in style from those that you use in your classroom. You may use these letters for the activities in this book or you can make your own copies of letter styles with which your students are most familiar.

Rewards and Recognition

Duplicate the awards, cut out and give to children during and/or at the conclusion of your alphabet activities. Be sure every student is given one or more awards.

YOU'RE A–OK

Great job!

Congratulations!

I'm proud of

_____

who knows the alphabet!

☆ **GOOD WORK!** ☆

_____

has done a special job with
the alphabet activities!